An impossible goodbye . . .

"Gus can't stay at the zoo forever," Justin told Jessica gently. "He's got to go back to the wild. His visit was only temporary."

Jessica burst into tears. The grizzly cub stirred in her lap.

Justin looked embarrassed. "I'll be back in a little while," he said softly, leaving the office.

Jessica sobbed into Gus's fur, and he whimpered. "I know. It's not fair, is it?" she asked him through her tears. "Nobody gets it. How do they expect me to just give you up?"

SWEET VALLEY TWINS
◇ SUPER EDITION ◇

Jessica's Animal Instincts

Written by
Jamie Suzanne

Created by
FRANCINE PASCAL

BANTAM BOOKS
NEW YORK·TORONTO·LONDON·SYDNEY·AUCKLAND

RL 4, 008-012

JESSICA'S ANIMAL INSTINCTS
A Bantam Book / June 1996

*Sweet Valley High® and Sweet Valley Twins® are
registered trademarks of Francine Pascal*

Conceived by Francine Pascal

*Produced by Daniel Weiss Associates, Inc.
33 West 17th Street
New York, NY 10011*

Cover art by James Mathewuse

ISBN: 0-553-48391-9

Published simultaneously in the United States and Canada

Bantam Books are published by Bantam Books, a division of Bantam
Doubleday Dell Publishing Group, Inc. Its trademark, consisting of the
words "Bantam Books" and the portrayal of a rooster, is Registered in the
U.S. Patent and Trademark Office and in other countries. Marca
Registrada. Bantam Books, 1540 Broadway, New York, New York 10036.

PRINTED IN THE UNITED STATES OF AMERICA

OPM   0 9 8 7 6 5 4 3 2 1

To Julian Decluat

One

"Two more weeks till summer vacation," Jessica Wakefield groaned. It was a Friday afternoon in June, and she was looking through the pantry for a snack.

Jessica's older brother, Steven, raised an eyebrow at her. "What are you talking about? Today was your last day of school, remember?" He took a bite of his enormous sandwich. "It's vacation already."

"Maybe for you, but not for me," Jessica muttered, pulling out the peanut butter. "I have to do my internship." Sixth and seventh graders at Sweet Valley Middle School could spend the first two weeks of vacation working at a business, and Jessica had signed up for the program this year.

"You?" Steven frowned. A gob of jelly fell out of his sandwich and landed on his shirt. "Since when do *you* give up vacation time to do a little extra work?"

Jessica sniffed. "Since when did *you* learn to eat like a pig?" she retorted. "Oh, excuse me, I guess you always have."

Steven wiped the jelly from his shirt. It left a purple streak. "For your information, fluff brain—"

"It just so happens," Jessica said quickly, cutting him off, "that all of us really cool kids in school are doing an internship—me, Lila, Mandy, Tamara." She ticked off names of some of the most popular girls in the school. Like Jessica, they all were members of the exclusive Unicorn Club. "Plus, we all get a pizza party. And it gives me a head start toward my career in the fashion industry."

"The fashion industry?" Steven repeated, grinning. "So you'll be modeling for Dracula movies?"

Jessica glared at him. *Brothers!* "No, I have different interests, thank you very much." She rummaged in the pantry again and found a bag of mini marshmallows.

"Oh, I see." Steven nodded seriously. "Like what? Sorting clothes at the dump? No, I take it back," he said as Jessica started to interrupt. "You'll be an intern at the circus and learn how to put on clown makeup. Then maybe they'll turn you into a human cannonball. Whoosh!" He arched his arm through the air and smashed it hard against the counter. "Blam! Just make sure they put in *plenty* of gunpowder, OK?"

Narrowing her eyes, Jessica picked up a marshmallow and aimed it at her brother's head. "I'm going to work for the Society for Sisters Who Can't Stand Their Idiotic Brothers."

"Must be a pretty small organization," Steven commented with a snort.

Jessica grit her teeth. *Be mature,* she commanded herself. *He's nothing but a dumb little boy, after all.* The fact that she was a twelve-year-old sixth grader and he was already in high school had nothing to do with anything. Inside, Jessica knew, she was much more mature than Steven. "Actually," she continued, forcing a smile onto her face, "would you like to know what I am doing for *my* internship?"

"Not really." Steven pretended to stifle a yawn.

"Well, I'll tell you anyway." Jessica tucked a few marshmallows into her peanut butter. "I'll be working with makeup. I applied to Sweet Valley Makeovers down at the mall. This time Monday I'll be putting foundation on some woman who just doesn't know how to do it right."

Steven hooted. "You?"

"Yeah," Jessica said, putting her hands on her hips. The idea of working with makeup almost made up for missing two weeks of summer vacation. Fashion was one of her favorite things.

She could see herself now, frowning down at a rich customer. "I think you ought to use a little more blush, ma'am," she'd say, "and perhaps a slightly darker shade of eyeshadow." "Do you really think so?" the customer would ask doubtfully. "Listen to Jessica," her boss, Mrs. Fiske, would say. "She knows what she's doing!" And after Jessica had finished her work, the customer would be totally blown away by how good she looked. She'd give Jessica a huge tip and recommend her to all her friends and—

"Aliens have claimed my sister," Steven said in a mournful voice, cutting into Jessica's thoughts. "*My* sister would have done cartwheels down the stairs when *she* found out she got the job she wanted. *My* sister would have told everybody over and over what an awesome experience this was going to be," he went on, changing to a squeaky falsetto. "The sister *I* know and hate would never let me get to Friday without hearing about her internship that starts Monday. And I haven't heard a single solitary word from this person over here." He shook his head. "So what planet are *you* from, huh?"

Jessica rolled her eyes. "Well, they haven't actually gotten back to me yet," she admitted, setting another slice of bread on the peanut butter. *Yum, a peanut butter and marshmallow sandwich.* "But I'm sure I'm in."

"Oh, you're sure, huh?" Steven blinked hard and set down his sandwich. "And the internship begins on Monday?" He shook his head. "Now I *know* you're an alien."

"What are you talking about?" Jessica snapped.

Steven leaned back in his chair. "When you've been around as long as *I* have," he said grandly, "you learn a few things about the way the world works. Like Rule Number One. Rule Number One says that if you want to start working at a makeup place on Monday, and you haven't heard from them by Friday, you *probably* didn't get the job."

"Get real." Jessica shot her brother an exasperated look, but she felt the slightest twinge of worry. Maybe she should have sent the application out earlier. Maybe she should have called first. Maybe—

"How long ago did you apply, anyway?" Steven wanted to know.

"Um . . ." Answering "Yesterday" didn't make Jessica seem mature and responsible, somehow. "A while ago," she said with a careless wave of her hand, as though it was so far back she couldn't even remember. "Maybe two weeks."

Steven shook his head. "You're such a *kid*. Don't you even know you're supposed to follow up your application with a phone call?"

"Sure I do!" Jessica's eyes blazed. She did, too. Only it was hard to follow up an application with a phone call if you weren't exactly sure when the application would arrive. "It's just that, um, Mrs. Fiske keeps being out of the office or something whenever I call." Which was true, Jessica reflected, as far as it went.

Steven's only answer was another snort.

"Well, she does!" Jessica insisted.

"All right, all right!" Steven put up his hands in mock surrender. "Forget I ever said anything. Just do me one favor, huh, Jessica?"

"What?" Jessica asked suspiciously.

Steven's lips curled into a mischievous grin. "Don't even *think* about giving *me* a makeover."

Now it was Jessica's turn to snort. She could imagine nothing worse. "OK," she agreed. "You're on!"

"Jessica! Guess what!"

Jessica's twin sister, Elizabeth, burst into the kitchen, panting. "I've got incredible news!" she gasped, leaning against the counter. "You'll never believe it!"

Jessica chewed her sandwich thoughtfully. "What is it?"

"I rode all the way home as fast as I could so I could let you know!" Elizabeth exclaimed.

Jessica widened her eyes. "Is Johnny Buck coming to town?" she asked hopefully. *Or is it something typically Elizabeth,* she wondered, *like the library will be building a new wing?*

Though the two girls looked exactly alike, with long blond hair, blue-green eyes, and a dimple in one cheek, they were very different people. They had their own sets of friends and their own interests. While Jessica loved fashion and soap operas, Elizabeth was happiest curled up with a good book.

In spite of their differences, the two girls were the best of friends. But Jessica couldn't always get excited about some of the things Elizabeth liked best.

Elizabeth smiled and caught her breath. "Better than Johnny Buck. It's so awesome, Jess. We won the lottery!"

"The lottery?" Jessica gasped. Her heart began to beat three times faster, even though she couldn't remember actually buying a ticket. "We won the *lottery?*" *We're going to be rich!* she told herself with excitement. *I'll buy a completely new wardrobe—and take trips all over Europe—and—*

"The state lottery?" Steven asked in disbelief. He set his sandwich down. "*You* two?"

"Not *that* lottery," Elizabeth said impatiently. Her eyes sparkled. "The school lottery. You know, Jess, the one for the internships."

The one for the internships? "Not the money lottery?" Jessica asked in a disappointed voice.

Elizabeth laughed. "Of course not, silly."

"Oh." Jessica's heart slowed to an ordinary pace. Her dreams of new clothes, travel, and riches— gone.

Steven swallowed the last bite of his sandwich. "You guys couldn't win the lottery anyway. You're too young. You have to be an adult. Now, I could probably pass for twenty-one, but you guys—" He rolled his eyes. "You're just kids."

"So what did we win?" Jessica asked loudly, trying to ignore her brother.

Elizabeth's face lit up. "It's so amazing, Jess," she said. "We've been chosen to work at the zoo!"

"At the zoo?" Jessica repeated in disbelief. "What do you mean, that's so amazing? I don't *like*—"

"There were about fifty kids who wanted to do it," Elizabeth continued breathlessly. "But they only had space for four, so they had to do a lottery. All of my friends wanted it so badly, and so did that kid in homeroom who wants to be a lion tamer, and that girl who swam with dolphins once when we were in, like, second grade—" She ran out of air. Clutching Jessica's hand, she breathed in deeply. "But they pulled out *our* names, Jess!" she continued. "I was just over at school and I found out—it's us and Melissa McCormick and Bruce Patman! And I'm giving a presentation about my experience just before the pizza party for the interns! Can you believe it?"

"Actually, no," Jessica said dryly, yanking her hand away. "How did my name get onto the list of people who wanted to be interns at the *zoo*, I'd like to know?"

Elizabeth didn't seem to be listening. "I'm so excited," she said with a grin. "I'll do anything they want me to do, of course. But I really, really hope I can work with baby animals." She sighed blissfully. "Maybe they'll put me in with leopard cubs, or something."

Baby leopards! Good grief! Jessica thought scornfully. She waved her hand in front of her sister's face. "E-*liz*-a-beth!"

"Or baby seals," Elizabeth went on dreamily. "Or fawns. I wonder if there are newborn fawns this time of year?"

Steven snickered. "Look!" he said, pointing his index fingers straight up from his head. "I'm a wittle newborn fawn! All I do evewy day is hop, hop, hop!" He put a goofy grin on his face and jumped across the kitchen. Batting his eyelashes, he wiggled his "antlers" at Elizabeth. "Will you take care of me, Mrs. Bambi?" he asked.

Jessica couldn't stand it anymore. "Be quiet, Steven!" Then she turned and gripped Elizabeth by the shoulders. "Elizabeth!" she snarled. *"How did my name get on that list?"*

Elizabeth reached out to steady herself against

the counter. For the first time she seemed to focus her eyes on Jessica. "Well—I put it there," Elizabeth admitted.

"Oh," Jessica said, unable to hold back her sarcasm. "And you didn't think maybe I might want to know?"

Elizabeth smiled tentatively. "I planned it as a surprise," she said. "I didn't really think we'd be picked, but I thought it would be such a thrill if we were." She cleared her throat. "I knew you'd love the zoo, and I wasn't sure you'd get around to signing up yourself."

"You knew I'd love the zoo?" Jessica repeated incredulously. "What planet are you from, anyway?"

"Hey, that's *my* line," Steven interrupted.

"Well, you *used* to like the zoo," Elizabeth explained. Her eyes nervously explored Jessica's face. "We always enjoyed going there when we were younger. Remember?"

"The key word is *younger*," Jessica spat out, waving her sandwich in the air to emphasize her point. "Zoos are horrible, smelly, disgusting places."

"But the animals—" Elizabeth began.

"I don't *like* animals!" Jessica dropped her sandwich onto the counter. "I don't like *dogs!* I don't like *cats!* I don't even like *gerbils!*"

"The gerbil exhibit at Sweet Valley Zoo," Steven said in a monotone, "is the envy of zoos worldwide. Three thousand, nine hundred and twenty-six gerbils live in a twelve-story apartment building with bathtubs, cable TV, and the world's largest—"

"Oh, cut it out," Jessica snapped, then glowered

at her sister. "I don't even like baby *rabbits*."

"Oh," Elizabeth said in a small voice. "So, um, I guess you're not totally happy about what I did?"

"You want an honest answer?" Jessica didn't wait for her sister's response. "No way!"

Elizabeth stared at the sandwich in front of her. For the last ten minutes, she had been sitting at the dining room table with Jessica and Steven, but she hadn't managed to take even a nibble yet.

I sure messed this one up, she told herself miserably. She had to admit, she'd been so excited over the thought of getting to work with Jessica, she hadn't stopped to think about what her twin might want. She looked at Jessica cautiously. "I'm really sorry, Jess," she ventured.

"You'd better go right back to school and take my name off that list," Jessica snapped, folding her arms across her chest.

Elizabeth frowned. She *did* feel badly, but she didn't see why Jessica had to be so stubborn. "Well, it's not like you had anything else planned," she argued. "I've been thinking about this for weeks and weeks, and you haven't done anything. If I hadn't put down your name, you wouldn't have an internship at all."

"Oh, that's not true," Jessica said impatiently. "I applied to Sweet Valley Makeovers almost a whole month ago!"

"Funny," Steven observed. "You told me it was two weeks."

"You stay out of this!" Jessica demanded, whirling to face her brother. "Two weeks, a month—who cares?"

Steven shrugged. "You're right," he said with a grin. "Two weeks living with Jessica sure seems like a month. Maybe even a year. Yuk, yuk, yuk." He bit into an apple with a loud crunch.

"But you don't know about the makeovers internship for *sure* yet?" Elizabeth pressed.

Jessica looked slowly at the floor. "Nope," she admitted.

"Then come on to the zoo," Elizabeth suggested, as brightly as possible. "We'll have fun. We can ride our bikes together. We can, um—" She thought hard. "We can compare notes about the animals we work with. Maybe we'll even get to work in the same habitat!" Suddenly she was feeling enthusiastic again. "Just think, Jess—we'll remember this experience for the rest of our lives!"

Jessica stared hard at her sister. "That's exactly what I'm afraid of!"

"I'm really sorry, Jess," Elizabeth said again as she wrapped her sandwich up and put it in the refrigerator a few minutes later. "I didn't think. I—I—I should have asked you what you wanted first. I—I'm sorry."

Jessica could tell that her sister *was* sorry, but that didn't make her any less angry.

"Yeah, right," Jessica said, slamming her half-eaten sandwich into the garbage. Suddenly, she wasn't hungry any more.

"I—I—I'm sorry," Steven mimicked, snapping open the lid on a can of soda. "I'm sorry for cutting your head off. I—I should have asked you what you wanted first."

Elizabeth bit her lip. "It's just that I figured—" She shrugged. "I guess I should have told you."

"Uh-huh," Jessica said dryly.

"I just thought we'd have a good time together," Elizabeth went on. Her voice sounded strained. "Isn't there some animal you'd like to be with—elephants, maybe, or something?"

Jessica considered. Elephants didn't bite you or jump out of dark corners and terrify you. From what she'd seen, they kind of minded their own business. Could she work with them? Well, maybe.

"See?" Elizabeth's voice broke into Jessica's thoughts. "Elephants would really be OK, right? Come on, Jess," she pleaded. "We'd have fun—"

"As *if*," Jessica growled. She'd just remembered the problems with elephants. In her mind she imagined herself shoveling elephant poop out of huge smelly cages, cages full of elephants with ugly wrinkled skin and bad tempers. She could see one of them grabbing her with its trunk and—

Jessica shuddered and made a grab for the phone book. "I am *not* going to the zoo, no matter what!" Quickly she found the number for Sweet Valley Makeovers and dialed it. *No possible way am I working at the zoo*, she thought. *I'll say my application got lost in the mail. Or maybe I'll say an elephant ate it.* She listened to the phone ring.

"Are you *sure*, Jess?" Elizabeth looked wistful.

"Better believe it!" Jessica made a face at her sister, then sucked in her breath as someone picked up the phone.

"Hello, Sweet Valley Makeovers, Mrs. Blair speaking."

Jessica put on her most grown-up voice. "Mrs. Fiske, please."

"Mrs. Fiske?" Mrs. Blair sounded doubtful. "I don't think she's here right now."

Not there? Jessica thought, a sense of alarm rising in her throat. *She has to be there.* "Well, would you check, please? It's—" She dropped her voice to a whisper. "It's important."

Mrs. Blair paused. "All right. One minute."

Sappy mood music began to play. "On hold?" Steven asked scornfully.

Jessica shook her head. "Oh, really?" she said into the receiver. *Why give Steven the satisfaction of being right?* She grinned as though someone had just said something funny. "Uh-huh." She paused for a few seconds. "Is that right?"

Mrs. Blair picked up the receiver again. "I'm sorry. Mrs. Fiske is out."

Jessica's face fell. "When—when will she be back?"

"Not today," Mrs. Blair said. "And she's off weekends. So the earliest you could get her would be Monday morning. Would you like to leave a message?"

Monday morning? Jessica bit her lip. Now what?

"Hello?" Mrs. Blair sounded irritated.

"Oh!" Jessica caught herself. "Um—do you happen to have Mrs. Fiske's home phone number handy?" she asked, hoping she sounded mature.

"I'm sorry, but we do not give out home phone numbers for the staff." Mrs. Blair's voice oozed disapproval.

"Oh," Jessica said blankly. She stared at the receiver in her hand. Maybe if she asked very nicely—"Oh. Um—please?"

"Is there a message?" Mrs. Blair snapped.

Jessica sighed. "No. No message. Thanks," she said, and hung up.

"No, huh?" Elizabeth sounded sympathetic.

"Told you you should have followed up your application earlier," Steven said, stuffing a huge handful of marshmallows into his mouth.

"She's gone home early." Jessica couldn't believe her bad luck. She sighed miserably. "I guess I'll be at the zoo on Monday after all." She could see the giraffes stepping on her—the lions sinking their sharp claws into her body—even the chinchillas nibbling her to death.

Elizabeth smiled. "I think you'll have fun," she predicted. "I really do."

"In your dreams." Jessica decided to call Mrs. Fiske Monday morning right at the stroke of nine. *No, make that 9:01. Give her time to get settled at her desk.*

"So the two of you will be working together, huh?" Steven said, wiggling his eyebrows and grinning evilly. "I always did say you guys belonged in a zoo!"

"Steven!" Jessica shouted.

Grabbing the marshmallow bag from the counter, she chased her brother out of the kitchen, pelting him with mini marshmallows all the way.

Two

"Jessica!"

Frantically Elizabeth shook her sister's sleeping form. It was Monday morning, nearly time for their internship to begin, and Jessica was still in bed.

"Jes-si-ca!" Elizabeth bellowed into her twin's ear. "If you don't hurry, we'll be late!"

Jessica opened one eye. "So what's the big rush, huh, Elizabeth?" Groaning, she closed her eye.

Elizabeth took a deep breath and looked at Jessica's digital clock. "Jessica, if you don't get out of bed right now, I'll leave without you," she threatened.

Jessica's eye flashed open once more. "Hurray," she said primly. "See you later. Have fun with the crocodiles."

"But Jess—" Elizabeth pleaded. She glanced around the room until her eyes lit on the head of a stuffed bear, buried under a pile of clothes in

Elizabeth's closet. *Aha!* "Get up right this minute or I'll tell everyone you still sleep with your teddy bear."

"Huh?" Jessica struggled to a sitting position. "I do not either! I haven't slept with Gus in, like, eight years!"

Elizabeth covered her grin. "Maybe not," she said. "But I'll tell everybody anyway."

"Don't you dare!" Jessica hopped out of bed.

"Meet me in ten minutes, and you've got yourself a deal," Elizabeth said. *All's fair in love and war,* she thought, a twinkle in her eye as she walked downstairs.

And all's fair in getting your sister to her internship on time!

Bruce Patman leaned against a red brick wall near the entrance to the zoo and surveyed the group of interns. It was nine o'clock on Monday, and he was impatient to get started. *Yup,* he thought happily, his eyes roving from Jessica to Elizabeth. *This is gonna be all right.*

Then he raised his eyebrows in Melissa McCormick's direction.

Oh boy, is it ever!

Bruce thought back to last Friday, when he'd heard he'd gotten the zoo internship. At first he'd been bummed out about being the only guy. But now that he thought about it, he was just as happy this way. *Bruce and the Three Babes,* he thought, running a hand slowly through his hair.

The head zookeeper smiled at the interns. "I'm

Mrs. Tomlinson," she began, "and I'd like to welcome the four of you here to the zoo. Please pay
careful attention to our rules. One, no feeding the
animals without permission from the keepers—"

Bruce let his eyes drift toward Melissa. *The
Wakefield twins are OK*, he thought. *If you like that
sort of thing. But Melissa!* He gave a low whistle. *Is
she hot, or what?* He'd always kind of admired her,
but lately his stomach had been doing cartwheels
whenever she walked by.

"And absolutely no teasing the animals," Mrs.
Tomlinson was saying. "Any questions so far?"

Bruce looked around at the three girls. Melissa
and Elizabeth were shaking their heads. Jessica, for
some reason, was leaning against a post, her face
sullen and angry.

"Good enough." Mrs. Tomlinson pulled out a
pad. "Now, two of you will be working together in
one of the habitats. I have your assignments right
here." She frowned at the paper in front of her.
"Oops, sorry. Wrong pad." Bending over, she rummaged through a briefcase at her feet.

Two of us together! Bruce lifted his eyebrows and
considered the possibilities. *They wouldn't put the
twins together*, he decided. *Which means one of those
two people could easily be me.*

He grinned happily. *Maybe it's me and Melissa*, he
thought, flashing her what he hoped was a really
cool wink.

Bruce and Melissa, he thought, trying the phrase
out on his tongue for size.

Way cool. Way, way cool.

*   *   *

"Let's see—" Mrs. Tomlinson grabbed another pad. "Ah. Here we are." She turned to Jessica.

"What do you want?" Jessica grumbled. She knew she was making a bad impression, but she didn't care. Even at the entrance to the zoo, the smell was already overpowering, and in the distance she was sure she could hear loud screams. *Probably keepers being dragged off by huge meat eaters.*

"We'll start with you." Mrs. Tomlinson sized up Jessica with a frown. "You'll be working with the bears."

"With the *bears?*" Jessica's mouth hung open.

"Bears," Mrs. Tomlinson confirmed.

Jessica couldn't believe her ears. Bears were worse than almost anything else she could think of. Except bats. And lions. And maybe pythons, or poisonous iguanas. But bears were pretty terrible, that was for sure. She glared at Mrs. Tomlinson. "There must be some mistake."

"No mistake." Mrs. Tomlinson peered at her paper once more, just to be sure.

"Bears *kill* people," Jessica went on in a loud voice. "They—they knock people over with their paws." She waved her arm like a mad grizzly. "They dig their claws into people. They *bite*. You don't want a little intern hanging around deadly animals, do you?" She made her voice sound small and weak. "I mean, *do* you?"

Mrs. Tomlinson blinked very rapidly.

"Maybe you'd like me to work in the office where it's really safe," Jessica suggested in a hopeful voice.

And where I can make a quick phone call or two, she added silently.

Mrs. Tomlinson smiled tightly. "Don't worry, dear. Justin Marx is head of our bear habitat, and he's very careful. I promise he won't let you get hurt. Now, Elizabeth—" she continued before Jessica had a chance to respond.

Jessica tuned out. *Good thing my dad's a lawyer*, she thought, gritting her teeth.

If I get eaten before I can call Mrs. Fiske, he'll sue the zoo for seven gazillion dollars!

"The monkeys?" Elizabeth could hardly believe her good fortune. "I'm going to get to work with *monkeys?*"

"Now that's more like it," Mrs. Tomlinson said heartily. "That's the kind of reaction we want our interns to have." She shot Jessica a brief glance, then grinned at Elizabeth. "I bet you'll have a blast."

Elizabeth smiled back. "Oh, I'm sure I will, Mrs. Tomlinson," she said. "Monkeys are so cute. And they're so much fun to watch, too." She remembered countless hours at the zoo when she was younger, nose pressed to the monkey cage, watching as the monkeys ran around, chattered, and swung all over the place. It was better than any TV show.

"The head keeper at the monkey house is Madeleine Turner," Mrs. Tomlinson told her. "She's wonderful—as good as Justin," she added in a loud voice, staring straight at Jessica, who didn't look up.

"I'm sure I'll learn a lot from her," Elizabeth said. She nudged her sister, who gave her a stony look.

Elizabeth sighed. Not even her twin's ugly mood could keep her spirits down for long. In her mind's eye she saw herself in the monkey cage, immediately accepted by a whole troop of monkeys. She'd be practically part of the group, just hanging out in their cage all day long and doing everything they did. The little babies would love her most of all, and she'd spend hours rocking them and putting them to sleep. She'd be just like their big sister, or something. *It'll be like babysitting,* she thought happily. *Only better, because monkeys are all furry.*

"All *right!*" Bruce exclaimed, pumping his fist into the air, when he heard Elizabeth's assignment.

Mrs. Tomlinson smiled. "I'm glad you're so happy for your friend, Bruce."

"Huh?" Bruce raised his eyebrows.

Mrs. Tomlinson frowned. "I'm glad you're—"

"Oh, yeah." Bruce nonchalantly kicked a pebble and jammed his hands into his pockets. "That's me—always happy for my friends." Elizabeth was looking at him strangely, but Bruce decided to ignore her. He didn't want to say what was really on his mind. If Jessica was with the bears, and Elizabeth was assigned to the monkey house, then that left just two people.

Himself. And Melissa.

Which meant they'd be working together!

"All right," Mrs. Tomlinson continued. "Bruce and Melissa, you two will be working together in the aviary."

Bruce grinned. *Yup*, he thought with satisfaction, drawing himself up to his full height and trying to look as cool as possible. *Just the way I wanted it.*

He threw Melissa a glance that he hoped looked man-of-the-world. Unfortunately, she just stared back at him, confusion all over her face.

Well. He could work on a really cool look later. After all, he'd have two weeks. Two whole weeks to impress her.

Ought to be a snap, he figured. Hey, the way girls fell all over him at school, he'd probably have to fight her off by the end of the third day. No, make that the second.

"You'll find that habitat by the rest rooms on the south side of the zoo," Mrs. Tomlinson went on.

"I'm sorry, ma'am," Bruce said in a chivalrous tone, raising a finger the way the hero had done it in a movie he'd seen once. "Just where did you say we would be working?" He flashed another glance toward Melissa. "I didn't catch it the first time, exactly."

Mrs. Tomlinson looked up from her notebook. "The aviary," she repeated.

"Oh. The aviary. Of course." Bruce nodded as though he spent all his spare time in the aviary. Whatever that was. *Aviary, aviary. Was that maybe where a beaver lived? Or—wait a minute, wasn't an aviary an airline pilot?* He frowned.

No, that was an "aviator."

Bruce tried hard not to look confused. He didn't want Melissa to know he'd never heard of an aviary. "Um—who's the head aviator? I mean—"

Bruce hesitated as Elizabeth and Melissa exchanged amused glances. *What are they laughing at?* he wondered. "That is," he went on casually, "who is our head keeper?" There. That was safe.

"Pamela Moreland," Mrs. Tomlinson said.

"Ah." Bruce nodded as though it was all suddenly clear. Four nods, five. *How many times does a really cool hero nod, anyway?* He decided to watch that movie again tonight to find out.

"Questions?" Mrs. Tomlinson snapped her notebook shut.

Melissa cleared her throat. "Yeah," she said shyly, raising her hand. "Um—what's an aviary?"

Mrs. Tomlinson smiled and turned to Bruce. "Why don't you tell her?"

"Me?" Bruce swallowed hard.

"Certainly," Mrs. Tomlinson said. "I'm sure a smart boy like you knows the answer."

Bruce gritted his teeth. He hated being called a "smart boy." "Um, well," he floundered, wishing he had just gone ahead and asked the question himself. His mind raced. "Um," he said again, stalling for time. *Aviary. Sounds like library,* he thought desperately. *If a library is run by a librarian, then—* "Avians live in an aviary, I guess."

Melissa and Elizabeth burst out laughing.

"What's so funny?" Bruce demanded angrily.

Melissa grinned. "What's an avian, Bruce?" she teased.

"Um—" To his horror, Bruce could feel his face turning bright red.

"Bruce is quite right." Mrs. Tomlinson's voice snapped them all back to attention. "An aviary is a place for 'avians'—for birds. 'Avian' is a fancy name for 'related to birds,' that's all." She beamed at Bruce. "What a smart boy."

"Yeah, well." Bruce grinned at Melissa. "Now you know," he added, nodding suavely. At least, he hoped it was suavely.

"Oh, birds!" Melissa gave a little cry of delight. "I *love* birds! Don't you?"

"Oh, yeah, I—" *Birds.* Suddenly Bruce realized what Melissa was saying. His jaw hung open.

And his knees began to buckle.

"Are you all right, Bruce?" Melissa stared at him curiously.

"J-just fine," Bruce blurted out, trying to steady himself against the brick wall behind him. In the distance a lion roared, but he barely noticed.

Birds! he thought again, as cold rivers of sweat trickled down the back of his neck.

For as long as Bruce could remember, he'd been afraid of birds. *Well, maybe not afraid, exactly,* he told himself as he struggled back to a standing position. *Worried about birds. Concerned about birds. Birds make me—uneasy, that's all.*

"You're positive you're all right?" Melissa asked doubtfully. "Anything I can do?"

"No." Bruce tried hard to push a picture out of his mind. A picture of an enormous hawk whooshing down from the stratosphere, wings beating six zillion times a minute, seizing Bruce with razor-sharp claws and carrying him into the air while Bruce screamed and screamed—"I mean," Bruce added, "no, thank you." He tried hard to concentrate on Melissa's face, hoping it would make the image of the bird disappear.

"All right." Melissa stepped back. "You just look a little sick, that's all."

"Well, I'm *not*." Bruce spoke forcefully. He stared intently at Melissa. *Good*. The picture was fading.

Melissa took another step back. "Why are you staring at me?"

Was I staring at her? "I'm not staring at you!" Bruce insisted, quickly looking down to the ground. *Oops*. Not ten feet from them a sparrow was hopping around. Bruce grimaced and turned away, but not before another vision flashed into his mind. This time a huge flock of birds, all looking just like that sparrow, came flying over all at once, and then they grabbed him and brought him back to their nest, which was as big as a condominium. Then they started pecking him to death with their razor-sharp beaks—

"Bruce?" Melissa's voice sounded very far away.

With a start Bruce looked back at her. Slowly he managed a smile. *Maybe I should ask if I can work with different animals*, he thought for a moment. But he dropped the idea. *If you switched, you wouldn't get to work with her*, he reminded himself.

"Are you really all right?" Melissa put her hands on her hips and frowned at him.

"Just fine," Bruce said, hoping he sounded totally calm and collected. "Hey, don't worry about me. I'm OK. No problemo."

Three

◇

Jessica leaned back against the brick wall and closed her eyes, hoping to shut out all the sights and sounds—and smells—of the zoo. *This is awful*, she thought. *I'm working with bears, Melissa and Elizabeth are giggling like a couple of third graders, and the place smells like—like—*

She filled her lungs with air.

Like a zoo, she completed, almost gagging.

At least, she thought miserably, *it can't get any worse.*

"Just a few more details," Mrs. Tomlinson said. "To show that you're authorized staff members, you'll need to wear a uniform. Here's a sample." Rummaging in her briefcase, she brought out a pair of coveralls.

"Oh, wow," Elizabeth said, her eyes shining.

"Cool," Melissa commented.

Gag! Jessica thought, staring in disbelief at the

coveralls in Mrs. Tomlinson's hand. The clothing was one piece and almost completely shapeless. A zipper ran from the collar to near the belt, and the legs seemed to go on and on forever. The Sweet Valley Zoo logo was in one corner—a cartoon penguin riding an elephant. But even that wasn't the worst of it.

"Puke green," she said aloud. "Oh boy. My favorite color."

Elizabeth frowned at Jessica. "Well, I think they're cute," she said.

Jessica sighed loudly. "Mrs. Tomlinson, we don't *have* to wear these outfits—do we?"

"I'm afraid you do, Jessica," Mrs. Tomlinson replied. "It's one of our rules."

Great. Jessica scowled and sunk lower against the wall. "But what if you don't have my size?" she asked hopefully.

"One size fits all," Mrs. Tomlinson told her in a cheery voice.

Jessica scowled again. She couldn't imagine wearing a tent like that. "It's not exactly fashionable," she pointed out.

Mrs. Tomlinson gave a brittle laugh. "Well, fashion isn't the idea at a zoo, Jessica. You wouldn't want to wear fancy clothes here."

Oh yeah? Wanna bet? Jessica thought.

"After all," Mrs. Tomlinson went on, "when you work at zoos, you get a little messy. I'm not wearing a uniform because I spend so much time in the office. But whenever I'm with the animals, I wear one, too."

"Can we keep our uniforms when we're done?" Melissa asked.

A puke green uniform, Jessica thought, shaking her head. *Every day for two weeks. And I'm surrounded by people who think this is absolutely as cool as you can get!*

She groaned and sank to the sidewalk.

Good thing I'm getting out of here—just as soon as I can call Mrs. Fiske!

"This is *so* exciting!" Melissa exclaimed as she and Bruce walked toward the aviary. "We're going to have a blast, I know it!"

Lady, you said a mouthful, Bruce thought suavely. He smiled back at Melissa. "I believe you're right," he said in the deepest voice he could manage.

Melissa looked at him in surprise. "What's wrong with your voice?" she asked.

"Oh—nothing," Bruce said hastily, in a voice not quite so deep this time. "It'll be a blast, all right."

"These uniforms are so cool, don't you think?" Melissa went on. They were heading toward the aviary from the locker rooms, where they'd put on their coveralls.

"You bet," Bruce said with a wink. *Yours looks awfully good on you, anyway,* he thought. He cleared his throat. "I think yours, um, matches your eyes," he said.

Melissa looked down at her uniform. "It does?" she asked in a surprised voice.

"Well, you know," Bruce said, noticing the way Melissa's hair hung down over her face. "I mean, like, your uniform matches your hair, which kind of goes with your eyes. That's what I meant."

Melissa's eyes widened. "But the uniform's kind of green. And my hair—"

"Isn't green," Bruce filled in quickly. "Your hair's not at all green."

"Oh." Melissa reached up shyly and patted her hair. "Thanks," she went on, coloring slightly. "I think."

"Any time," Bruce assured her. *I bet I'd look more macho with the pants legs rolled down over my shoes,* he thought, stopping to adjust the uniform.

Melissa frowned. "Can you walk that way?"

"Oh, walk," Bruce said grandly, with a careless wave of his hand. He imagined himself walking out of the zoo at the end of the day with Melissa hanging adoringly on his arm. *"Oh, Bruce!"* she'd coo in his ear. *"You know the most amazing things!"*

Yup, he thought, his chest swelling ever so slightly. *Melissa McCormick and her boyfriend, Bruce "the Man" Patman!*

The smell was even worse inside the bear habitat. Jessica gagged as she walked into the building where the cages were kept.

"Oh, you'll get used to it," Justin said. A small, excitable man, he bounced ahead of Jessica, pointing out the bears in his care. "Here's the Kodiak cage, and over there are a couple of black bears. Which ones are you most interested in?"

"None of them, really," Jessica said.

"Oh." Justin seemed disappointed. "Well, I could

put you on technical jobs for now if you'd rather—mashing the food, hosing down the cages—"

Give me a break, Jessica thought frostily. *Speaking of which*—"When do I get a break?" Jessica asked.

Justin turned to her in surprise. "A *break?*" he asked, giving her a funny look. "You just got here."

"I know," Jessica said, studying her fingernails. She knew she wasn't exactly the star intern, but she didn't care what kind of impression she made on this guy. *As soon as I get my break I'll be history anyway*, she thought.

Justin opened his mouth, then closed it again. "Um—why don't you watch the polar bears for a little while first?" he suggested, motioning toward a pool at one end of the building. Jessica could see a few white bears lolling in the water. "Just observe for a few minutes," Justin went on. "Then we can talk about what you saw. *Then* we can talk about a break. OK?"

Boring. Jessica sighed. "OK," she agreed with a yawn.

I can do it. But I don't have to like it!

"Nice to meet you." Madeleine Turner, the head keeper at the monkey house, smiled at Elizabeth and extended her hand.

Elizabeth shook it vigorously. "I'm excited to be here," she said. She looked around the enormous building. "You have a ton of monkeys," she said, impressed.

"We certainly do." Madeleine gave a little laugh. "I think the total is sixty-three—but no one's counted for about a month." She pointed to a nearby cage. "See, those brown ones are Marcia and Jafiri, and the one that's a little larger is named Screeches, because that's what he does all day. And you can see Howler, Capuchin, Kiyesha, and Captain Spaulding, back to front."

Elizabeth watched the monkeys, who were moving rapidly around the cage.

"Kiyesha especially likes carrots," Madeleine went on. "And Capuchin and Marcia like to play practical jokes, and Howler's very musical."

"Musical?" Elizabeth strained to hear Madeleine over the din of sixty-three monkeys chattering and skidding from branch to branch. "How do you know?"

Madeleine smiled. "Oh, he'll sit for hours and listen to recordings," she explained. "He likes classical music pretty well, but he's especially fond of Johnny Buck."

Johnny Buck! Elizabeth thought, laughing at the idea of a monkey enjoying the songs of her favorite rock star. "You really have them listen to music?"

"Of course," Madeleine said. "Monkeys are very smart, you know. They have an incredibly complicated social system, and they communicate with each other like you wouldn't believe."

"Wow," Elizabeth murmured, watching the action.

"And there's Henry, and Henry the Second," Madeleine went on, pointing, "and Miss Milwaukee— she came from a zoo in Wisconsin—and Spanky's the little gray one."

Elizabeth shook her head. Spanky looked down at her curiously from the top of a tall tree. "How in the world can you tell them apart?" she asked as Spanky gave her a little wink and scampered down the tree.

"After a few days, it's easy," Madeleine promised. "They're all so different! It's one of the great things about monkeys."

"I bet," Elizabeth murmured. She took a step toward the cages. "I can't wait to get to know them myself!"

"So aren't they *neat?* What did you see?" Justin grinned at Jessica and pointed toward the polar bears.

"They didn't *do* anything," Jessica replied in her most bored voice. "They just sat there, that's all."

Justin's smile faded. "Didn't they swim?" he asked.

"Oh, swim," Jessica said dismissively. "Yeah, they swam, I guess."

"Well—how did they swim?" Justin pressed. "I mean, was it on their backs or on—"

Jessica shrugged and yawned.

Justin frowned. "Why don't you move up a little?" he asked, starting to steer Jessica closer to the cage.

Jessica dug in her heels. "I'm just fine back here," she told him in a clipped tone. *Back here where they can't reach. And where the smell might make me barf, but it won't kill me.*

"Oh. OK," Justin said, biting his lip. "Anyway,

isn't it interesting the way that big one keeps moving his head back and forth?"

"No," Jessica said with a careless shake of the head.

Justin's frown deepened. "Or the way the female uses her paws to push off underwater? You know, polar bears have been found twenty-five miles away from the nearest land. They're incredibly strong swimmers."

"That's nice." Jessica yawned as widely as she could.

"Which ones are your favorites?" Melissa turned to face Bruce. They were almost to the aviary.

"Huh?" Bruce answered. He had been thinking so hard about impressing Melissa, he hadn't quite heard the question. He gave an offhand shrug. "Oh, you know. This and that."

"Oh." Melissa gave him a strange look. "I like the cardinals best."

Bruce nodded knowingly. Finally, something he could really talk about—baseball teams. "Me, too," he said. "Well, I'm also a Dodger fan," he added quickly. "But the Cardinals—they're a pretty radical team. They've got some guys who can really hit."

Melissa stared at him, bewilderment all over her face. "What are you talking about?"

Bruce met her gaze. Something told him he'd made a mistake, but he couldn't figure out exactly what. "Well, you know," he said oh-so-casually. "This and that."

"My favorite *bird* is the cardinal," Melissa said, exaggerating the word so Bruce couldn't miss it. "That's what *I* was talking about."

"Oh," Bruce said quickly. "Of course. I knew it all along. My favorite is the—" *The Dodger,* he wanted to say, but he didn't. Instead, he searched his mind for the smallest, least dangerous bird around. "Um, the hummingbird," he said at last.

"Oh!" Melissa sighed happily. "I *love* humming-birds! The way their little wings beat over and over! They're so incredibly strong, and they have those sharp little beaks for gathering food. And they fly so fast, too!"

"Um—yeah," Bruce said weakly. He hadn't real-ized that hummingbirds were so, well, powerful. *Superbirds,* he thought glumly. With nice sharp beaks, too.

Bruce shook his head as they walked on. *Come on, Patman,* he chided himself. *A bird is a bird, that's all. There's a reason why we call dumb people "bird-brains," right? All you have to do is be smarter than a few birds for just two weeks—and you'll walk out of here with Melissa on your arm. Guaranteed.*

He quickened his pace. *Yeah, piece of cake,* he as-sured himself. *It's not like I've got any competition.*

I mean, how hard can it be to take her attention off a bunch of dumb birds—and get her to notice me?

"Well, how about the black bears?" Justin ven-tured, his mouth a tight line as he stared at Jessica. "Are you interested in them?"

Jessica shrugged.

"It's almost feeding time," Justin went on. "You can come in with me and see how it's done. Maybe by the end of the week you'll be able to do it by yourself."

Jessica stared at him in amazement, curling her lip.

"At the end of two weeks, then," Justin corrected himself. He hefted a huge bag of food. "So how about it?"

"No thanks," Jessica said. She sat down on a bench, pretended to look at her watch, and shut her eyes. "You go ahead. I'll just sit here and rest for a while."

"Oh, look!"

Outside the aviary, Melissa grabbed Bruce's arm and pointed. "Aren't they *darling?*"

Bruce tried hard to focus on Melissa's hand on his arm. But he couldn't. From overhead there came a loud shrieking noise. Without meaning to, Bruce looked up.

Straight up.

Oh, man. Suddenly Bruce was drenched with sweat. Up at the top of the aviary, a humongous hawk circled slowly. It was at least twice as big as any bird he'd ever seen.

Maybe three times as big.

Sucking in his breath, Bruce watched the hawk gliding through the air. When it turned, it seemed to balance on one wing. He could see its eyes glinting in the sunshine. His throat felt dry. *It's looking right at me.*

Bruce forced his gaze away from the hawk. But right nearby, three other huge birds sat perfectly motionless on a wooden plank at the very top of a long, skinny pole.

Bruce swallowed hard.

They, too, were staring directly at him.

"Come on, Bruce!" Melissa lifted the latch.

"Um—" Bruce struggled to speak. He stood stock-still, just staring at the predators on the plank above him.

"Bruce?" Melissa frowned. "Aren't you coming?"

"Um—later," Bruce hesitated. He backed away slowly, not daring to take his eyes off the birds. "I—I have to go to the bathroom."

"So what *do* you want to do?"

Jessica wished Justin would move away from her a little. Even though they were standing outside, a few yards away from the bear cages, Justin's uniform smelled faintly of what Jessica thought was bear poop.

"Oh, whatever," she said, studying her fingernails.

Justin pulled up a bucket, turned it upside down, and squatted on top of it. "You don't want to watch the polar bears, you don't want to feed the black bears. I assume you don't want to mop out the sun bear cage?"

Jessica shuddered. "Are you *kidding?*"

Justin sighed. "I didn't think so," he said. "Tell me, why are you here, anyway?"

Jessica studied her fingernails even harder. She

decided maybe she wouldn't bother to answer that question.

"All right." Justin leaned a little closer. "Suppose I let you do anything you wanted in the bear habitat. Anything at all. It could be here, or—" he looked meaningfully at Jessica "—it could be in the office. What would you do?"

The office! Jessica's heart leaped. "Something in the office, I guess," she said, trying not to sound excited. "I'm pretty good at filing papers. And making phone calls."

Justin fixed her with a look. "All right," he said slowly. "It's not exactly what I had in mind for an intern, but—" He hopped off the bucket. "Right this way, please."

Yes! Jessica thought, springing to her feet and following along.

Justin's office wasn't very big, but Jessica didn't mind. It was air-conditioned, no one could see her wearing her stupid uniform, and—best of all— there was a telephone right there on the desk. "Don't worry," she said, indicating the pile of papers Justin had given her to sort. "I'll take care of this. You'll probably want to get back to the bears, huh?" she added hopefully.

Justin frowned. "Uh-huh. Actually, though, I have a few things I wanted to check in the files."

Jessica resisted the urge to push him out of the office. "Later," she wheedled, and cocked her head as though she were listening very hard. "I think I hear one of the bears yelling."

Justin looked at her suspiciously, then shrugged. "All right. I'll check back in fifteen minutes." He headed out the door.

Jessica forced herself to wait till she couldn't hear the sound of his footsteps. Ten seconds—twenty—

Like a starving wolf attacking a piece of meat, Jessica grabbed the phone.

"Sweet Valley Makeovers, Mrs. Fiske."

First try! Jessica pumped her free hand into the air. "Hello, Mrs. Fiske," she said, hoping the smell of the zoo wouldn't carry over the phone lines. "This is Jessica Wakefield, from Sweet Valley Middle School? I sent you an application for an internship, like, a while ago?"

"I beg your pardon?" Mrs. Fiske sounded confused.

"Jessica Wakefield," Jessica said quickly. "About an internship?"

There was silence. "Oh, dear, no," Mrs. Fiske said after a moment. "We don't require new salespeople right now, oh, no."

"Oh, I don't want to be a salesperson," Jessica said quickly, afraid that Mrs. Fiske would hang up. "I mean, not the paid kind. I'm just a kid." Jessica bit her lip. "Um—that is, I'm a young woman eager to learn about the makeup business, and I'll work for free." Quickly Jessica tried to explain the internship program.

"Oh," Mrs. Fiske said after Jessica was done. "No, I didn't receive any application. And I doubt we'll be needing any extra help of any kind, not right now." Her voice became gentler. "But thank you for thinking of Sweet Valley Makeovers."

Jessica's heart nearly stopped beating. She gripped the receiver tightly. "No extra help?" she repeated, feeling dizzy.

"Not at this time."

"Can—can I at least leave my phone number?" Jessica asked weakly.

"Well, I suppose."

Jessica rattled it off, desperate.

"If something comes up, I shall certainly let you know," Mrs. Fiske promised.

"Can I call you tomorrow?" Jessica burst out. But the only answer was a click—and a dial tone.

Jessica stared at the phone in her hand. Now she really couldn't wait for three o'clock, when her day at the zoo would come to an end.

She had plans—serious plans—for the rest of the afternoon.

Four

Precisely at three that afternoon, Jessica stalked out of the zoo and unlocked her bike.

"Jessica!" Elizabeth called out behind her. "Wait up!"

Jessica glanced at her sister. *She's still wearing that stupid uniform!* she thought scornfully. "I'll wait for three minutes, that's it! You're going to change, I hope?" she added, pointing to the coveralls.

"Change?" Elizabeth shrugged. "Why would I want to change? I'm going to wear these home."

Jessica sighed loudly, totally exasperated. "Yeah, well, you would," she snapped, backing her bike out of the rack. No way in the world was she going to be seen riding home with someone who looked like *that*. "I'll catch you later."

Like on the twelfth of never! she thought grimly as she put her bike in gear.

*   *   *

The mall. Jessica sighed with satisfaction as she pulled her bike to a stop outside the front entrance. *Now this is where I belong*, she thought, hoping her clothes didn't have any traces of bear smell. She was determined to get a job at the mall—any job. *If Sweet Valley Makeovers can't use me—well, I'll find somebody who can!*

The mall was a busy place, as usual. Jessica wandered around for a few minutes, letting the voices of shoppers swirl around her ears. She stopped to look into a few display windows. No doubt about it: she felt like she'd come home. *Much nicer than the zoo*, she thought happily, walking by the frozen-yogurt store. *No messes to clean up, nobody growls at you, and best of all—the smells are good ones, things like perfume and cinnamon rolls!*

The only question was which stores to try—and in what order. Jessica was torn. "A jewelry store would be pretty cool," she said aloud. In her mind's eye she could see herself lifting precious stones out of a glass display case. The diamonds would sparkle in the gleam from the overhead lamps. Maybe they'd even let her try on a few of the most beautiful gems. *I bet sapphires would go well with my eyes*, Jessica thought.

On the other hand, Jessica wondered if she should try a trendy boutique first. *They might even let me model some stuff*, she said to herself. *Prom gowns—designer jeans—maybe even fur coats or something*. She imagined herself walking around the mall in a fancy dress that would cost a ton of money, smiling and nodding to everyone she saw.

Then, back at the store, she'd help customers choose clothes that would look almost as nice on them. Almost.

Then there was the cute gift shop. And the ear-piercing place where they sold snazzy earrings. And—Jessica sniffed the air delicately—the cinnamon-roll store might be a good choice, too.

Come to think of it, every place looked good. Except, of course, the pet store.

Jessica shook her head, grinning.

Decisions, decisions!

The cosmetic counter in the department store was nearly empty. A young woman looked up and smiled as Jessica stepped up to the display case. "Can I help you?" she asked.

"Um—yeah," Jessica said, extending her hand. She was pleased to see that the woman's name tag read WANDA: MANAGER. "I'm a student at Sweet Valley Middle School, and I need a placement for an internship."

"An internship?" Wanda shook her hand, a puzzled expression on her face.

"I'm very knowledgeable about perfume and makeup," Jessica went on, smiling broadly. "I've been interested in cosmetics for, like, my whole life, and I feel I could bring a lot to your, um, display area. I could learn a lot from you, too," she added hastily, in case Wanda might think she was stuck-up.

"An internship." Wanda smiled. "That's a real possibility. When would you be starting this?" She grabbed a piece of paper and a pencil. "I'd need to run it by the home office."

Home office? Jessica wondered what that was. She grinned broadly. "I could start tomorrow for sure."

"Tomorrow?" Wanda raised her eyebrows.

Jessica cleared her throat. Had she said something wrong? "Um, actually, I could start today, I guess, if you wanted me to. I just have to be home for dinner at six, but—"

Wanda held up her hand. "When would this internship end?" she asked curiously.

"Next week," Jessica told her cautiously. "Like, a week from Friday?"

"Oh, next *week*," Wanda sighed. She put the pencil down. "I'm sorry, dear. It would take at least two weeks for the home office to approve having you around."

"Oh," Jessica said in a small voice. "So—the answer's no?"

"I'm afraid so," Wanda told her, shaking her head. "I'm really sorry. I wish—" She hesitated. "There's nothing I can do now. I wish you'd come by two weeks ago, or even the week before that."

Jessica suppressed a groan. How could people expect her to think so far ahead?

EARS PIERCED: WHILE YOU WAIT.

Kind of a silly sign, Jessica thought with a grin, peering into the kiosk where a clerk was wrapping up a pair of fish-shaped earrings. *I mean, what am I going to do—leave my ears here while I go shopping someplace else?*

"Hello?" she asked timidly. The clerk turned to face her. "I'm looking for an internship program," she went on, "and I'm really interested in, um, jewelry, and, um, ears, and I would love to do my internship here."

"How old are you?" the clerk asked briskly, glancing at Jessica from head to foot.

How old? Jessica wondered if she should tell the truth, or not. "Um—does it matter?" she asked innocently.

The clerk nodded. "If you're not sixteen, you can't work here, period. Insurance. Or maybe it's the health department. I forget which." She frowned. "You're not sixteen, are you?"

"Yes, I'm sixteen," Jessica replied firmly before she knew what she was saying. She straightened her shoulders.

"Hmm." The clerk leaned forward. Jessica stuck out her chest and tried to look taller than usual. "Gee, I don't know—"

"Please," Jessica begged. "I, I really know a lot about ear piercing and—"

"What year were you born?"

"Huh?" Jessica stared at the clerk in confusion. "What do you mean, what year was I—"

"Answer the question," the clerk said. "Quick!"

Jessica opened her mouth to give the proper answer. Then she shut it again. *Sheesh.* Suddenly she understood why the clerk had asked. *If I tell her the real year, that will prove I'm twelve—but what year did you have to be born in so that you would be sixteen now?* "Um," Jessica said, pressing her hands to her temples and closing her eyes in an effort to concentrate. *Add four—no, subtract four—*

"Sixteen. Oh, sure." The clerk rolled her eyes. "Give me a break. You don't look a day over ten."

"Ten!" Jessica put her hands on her hips and stared angrily at the clerk. "What are you talking about? I turned twelve back in—"

She broke off. But as a smirk spread across the clerk's face, she realized it was too late.

"Lila! What are you doing here?"

Jessica stopped in her tracks right in the doorway of Briana Taylor's, the most exclusive clothing store in the mall. There in front of her stood her friend and fellow Unicorn Lila Fowler, arm draped over a rack of ball gowns.

"Jessica!" Lila exclaimed. Her eyes danced. "What are *you* doing here?"

"I asked you first." Jessica stared hungrily at the gowns. They were absolutely beautiful—especially the pale pink one with the plunging neckline. She wondered what it cost.

Lila beamed. "I'm working here."

"Working—*here?*" Jessica stared at her friend in astonishment. "At Briana Taylor's? You mean, for your internship?"

"That's right." Lila's smile grew wider. "There were, like, twenty kids who wanted the spot. But I won the lottery for it," she said proudly, motioning to the expensive clothing behind her. "Isn't it wonderful?"

"Wonderful," Jessica agreed, her heart sinking.

Even though she and Lila were best friends, the girls were extremely competitive with each other. Jessica couldn't stand it when Lila came out on top.

"They could only take one intern," Lila went on, "and it turned out to be *me!* Isn't that awesome? I'm going to buy a ton of these dresses." She swept her arm through the air grandly. "They're incredibly expensive, but Dad says price is no object." Lila's father was the richest man in Sweet Valley, and he gave Lila just about anything she wanted.

Jessica forced a smile. "That's great, Lila," she said, barely able to get the words out.

"Oh, hey, Jessica, what's your internship, anyway?" Lila asked, her eyes bright. "I don't think you ever told me."

"No?" Jessica pretended to be surprised. Stepping forward, she reached behind Lila and grabbed the price tag on the pale pink dress. *Two thousand dollars!* Dropping the tag as if it were diseased, she managed a weak smile and turned to leave the store.

"I hope it's not something stupid!" Lila called to Jessica's back. "We Unicorns have an image to keep up! It better not be a toy store, or the zoo, or something idiotic like that!"

Jessica stiffened, but she didn't break stride. "It isn't!" she yelled back over her shoulder.

It better not be for much longer, anyway!

Coming to a stop in front of the sporting goods store, Jessica reached down to rub her feet. It was almost six o'clock, and none of the stores she'd really wanted had been even a little bit interested.

Well, a sporting goods store is better than a zoo, she thought as she walked through the entrance. *I mean, they'll have volleyballs and Rollerblades and—*

A man dressed in a football uniform blocked her way. "Hup-one, hup-two, hup-three, hike!" he yelled. "Can I help you?"

"Um—I'd like to see the manager, please," Jessica said, feeling a little rattled. Above her, a pair of giant hands flashed onto a huge electronic message board and started to clap.

"The manager? You mean the coach!" The football player grabbed a whistle from the counter and blew a loud blast.

Another man ran out from a back room. He was wearing running shoes and held a large clipboard. The word COACH was written in big letters across his sweatshirt. The football player pointed to Jessica. "This young fan would like a word with you," he said, backing away. "I'm going to go tackle a few more customers."

Tackle the customers? Jessica looked around uneasily. "Um—" she began.

A woman in a basketball jersey appeared at the coach's side. "I've been on the floor for two hours straight," she moaned, rubbing her knee. "When does a sub go in for me, huh, Coach?"

The message board lit up with a monstrous "ST. LOUIS 7, PITTSBURGH 4."

The coach grabbed an antique car horn and squeezed it hard. The beep was deafening. "Amodeo in for Connors at salesperson!" he shouted into a microphone.

"Thanks," the woman sighed, limping toward the back room.

Jessica stared. *This is totally weird,* she thought. A young man in tennis whites darted from the back and sprinted toward a customer.

"At Sweet Valley Sporting Goods, you're always safe at home!" the coach shouted, extending a hand to Jessica. "Can I help you, ma'am?"

"Um—I don't think so," Jessica gasped as the message board above her flashed the words MAKE NOISE. Backing up, she felt her body knock into a display case. A golf club fell to the ground. Startled, Jessica bent to retrieve it.

"Tweet!" Jessica spun around. A woman in a black-and-white striped shirt stood nearby, standing on roller skates and blowing a whistle accusingly at Jessica. "Two minute penalty!" she announced. "Interference with merchandise!"

"Oh, sorry—here." Jessica dropped the golf ball, then turned around and began to run.

Somehow she had the feeling that a sporting goods store *would* be worse than a zoo after all.

One more try, Jessica thought grimly, checking her watch. *And this one better pan out.*

Because if it doesn't, I may be forced to kill my sister!

She walked quickly into the store right next to Sweet Valley Sporting Goods, not bothering to check what kind of store it was. "Hi," she said to the man behind the counter. She decided not to beat around the bush this time. "I need to work here for my internship. I can start tomorrow. OK?"

The man frowned. "I beg your pardon?"

Jessica sighed and repeated herself, more slowly this time.

"An internship." The man leaned forward thoughtfully. "That might be interesting."

Jessica's heart leaped. "I'm a really good worker," she went on. "I'll be here every day, and I'll do anything, I mean, like, anything." She flashed him a winning smile. "I really want to work here."

"Well, that certainly sounds good." The man shifted position in his chair. "What other qualifications do you have?"

Jessica waved her hand in the air. On the shelf behind the counter she could see a long row of books. "Oh, I'm really good with books. I read them all the time, and—"

"Books?" The man's mouth opened wide.

Oops. Jessica bit her lip. Now that she looked carefully at the shelf, she saw that the books weren't regular books at all—just ledgers and three-ring spiral binders. "I mean, computers," she said quickly, noticing a computer in a corner of the counter. "I've been doing computers since I was, like, two, and I really know tons about them, and—"

"Computers?" The man looked more confused than ever.

Uh-oh. "Um—what do you sell here, then?" Jessica asked, almost afraid to hear the answer.

The man frowned. "This is an insurance office," he said, exaggerating every word. He stood up and motioned through the doorway. "The bookstore is *there*," he said heavily. "And the computer store, I believe, is down the other way." He shook his head and put his hands on his hips. "Any other questions?"

Jessica slouched defeatedly. This insurance man definitely didn't look too interested in hiring her. "Yeah," she said. "Which way to the zoo?"

"So how was the zoo today?" Mrs. Wakefield handed a plate of garlic bread to Jessica at dinnertime. Jessica loved garlic bread, but she passed the plate on, glowering at it. She was too upset to even think about eating.

"Oh, Mom, it was so wonderful!" Elizabeth reached for the butter and the salt. "They've put me in with the monkeys!"

"Classic," Steven observed from the other side of the table. He chugged a glass of milk and poured himself another one. "My sister, the monkey. Oooh, oooh!" he chirped, scratching himself in the armpits. "Oooh, oooh! Hey, how long till you get like this?"

Jessica rolled her eyes and wished desperately that Steven would go away. Preferably to another galaxy.

Elizabeth smiled. "Cut it out, Steven."

"No, really," Steven insisted. "When do you get to start eating bugs like monkeys, huh? Slurp, slurp!" He pretended to find a few bugs in his spaghetti. "Delicious!"

Elizabeth leaned over and pointed to the carrot sticks on Steven's plate. "Actually, some of the monkeys at the zoo like these best." Her eyes twinkled.

"As *if*," Steven said dismissively. His face suddenly lit up. "Hey, I'll be a monkey's uncle! Get it?" he asked, looking around the table. "I will be! If Elizabeth's kids are monkeys, then I'd be a monkey's uncle, get it? Yuk, yuk! Get it?"

Jessica sighed impatiently. "Remind me to laugh sometime next week."

"How about you, Jessica?" Mr. Wakefield frowned down at Jessica's empty plate. "Here, have a little spaghetti, at least. How's the zoo treating you?"

Jessica gave the tiniest shrug she could.

"She's in the bear habitat," Elizabeth put in when Jessica didn't say anything.

"Bare?" Steven snapped in mock surprise. "My sister's taking off all her clothes so she'll be bare?" He made a face.

"Steven," Mr. Wakefield said reprovingly, serving Jessica some food.

Jessica looked at her brother with narrowed eyes, then forced a meatball into her mouth. "The only way I like animals is as food," she said, chewing slowly. *And as fur.*

"Oh, come on." Elizabeth grinned at her. "You'll feel differently in a few days, I promise."

"Yeah, I'll probably hate them even more." Jessica toyed with a strand of spaghetti. Nine more days of work at the zoo. Nine more days of torture. She shook her head.

Unless I can do something about it.

"Oh, kids, I had something I wanted to tell you." Mrs. Wakefield wiped her mouth on her napkin. "I'm working on a very important design project right now for some wealthy clients, Mr. and Mrs. Tweed." Mrs. Wakefield was an interior designer. "Mr. and Mrs. Tweed are—interesting people."

"That means they're difficult to deal with," Mr. Wakefield explained with a grin.

His wife smiled. "They're finicky. They like everything to be just exactly right."

"So what does this have to do with us?" Steven slurped down some more milk.

"Some of our meetings will be here at the house," Mrs. Wakefield went on. "So I need you three to be on your best behavior. And the house has to stay clean, too." She looked meaningfully at Jessica and Steven.

"Aw, Mom," Steven said, wrinkling his nose.

A thought suddenly whirled into Jessica's mind. "Hey!" she burst out before she could stop herself. "Maybe—Mom, could I, like, work with you for my internship? On your design project for the Tweeds, I mean?"

"Work with me?" Her mother looked surprised. "You'd want to work with me?"

Not really, Jessica thought. *But it would be tons better than the zoo!* "We'd have fun," she said aloud. "And we'd get to know each other a little better—"

Steven snorted.

"Well, we would!" Jessica snapped. "It'd be a real mother-daughter thing, Mom. You know how in the olden days mothers used to teach daughters how to sew and stuff like that. It would be just like back then. Please?"

Mrs. Wakefield smiled, but she shook her head.

Jessica's heart sank. "I don't think so, Jessica," she said at last. "If you'd like to help me for fun, that would be one thing. But for extra credit—" She sighed. "I'm sorry, dear. I just don't think that would be good for our relationship."

"Oh yeah?" Jessica didn't even try to hide her anger and disappointment. She stood up and banged her fist on the table. "And it will be good for our relationship for me to get shredded by a bunch of wild bears?"

Turning around before anyone could reply, she stomped away from the table and up to her room.

Five

Bruce gritted his teeth as he approached the aviary on Tuesday morning. *Today*, he promised himself, *I'm going to walk as far as the tree halfway across the cage.*

I think.

Yesterday he'd spent all his time at the edge of the aviary, near the flamingos, making up dumb excuses every time the keeper wanted him to go somewhere else. He hoped Melissa hadn't noticed. Flamingos were pretty goofy looking, but at least they didn't fly much. Or have sharp claws, or peck your eyes out.

"Come on in," Melissa said, smiling as she held the gate open for him.

"Thanks." Bruce swaggered in, trying to look as brave as possible. A crow cawed somewhere inside. Gently, Bruce leaned back against the chain-link fence. *Just in case*, he told himself.

"Are you feeling all right today?" Melissa asked anxiously.

"Of course I am." Bruce stepped forward and flexed a bicep. "I'm in great shape, hardly ever sick. Why do you ask?" He flexed the other bicep, too. *Might want to start hitting the weights every day for a while—*

"Oh, nothing." Melissa shrugged. "I was just wondering about your stomach."

"My stomach?" Bruce raised an eyebrow in what he hoped was a healthy kind of way. "What do you mean?"

"Just that you went to the bathroom about twelve times yesterday," Melissa said with a smile. She started to walk toward the other end of the aviary.

"Oh, *that!*" Bruce felt his face turn red with embarrassment. "Well, my stomach's just fine today," he said forcefully, but it was too late.

Melissa wasn't listening any longer.

Jessica retrieved her green coveralls from the corner of the locker room where she'd thrown them yesterday. She grimaced and put them on as slowly as she could. They smelled. The locker room smelled. In fact, the whole zoo smelled.

"Jessica?" Justin's voice came from outside the door.

"Coming!" Jessica slammed the door to her locker. Turning back to her backpack she pulled out the sweater and sweatpants she'd brought along. *There*, she thought as she yanked the sweater over her head and adjusted the sleeves. She studied her reflection in the mirror. *Ha. The green hardly shows.* Just in case, she pulled her collar up a little higher.

"Jessica! I need you!"

What could Justin possibly need me for? Jessica wondered, sliding the sweatpants over the legs of her uniform. "I'll be right there!" she called out, rolling her eyes. *Maybe he wants me to give one of the polar bears a makeover,* she thought, shaking her head. *That's about the only way I could be useful around here. Or—wait a minute—*

"Is it a phone call for me?" Jessica cried out, making sure no barf green showed over the tops of her shoes. Maybe it was Mrs. Fiske. Jessica had planned to call her later on, but if she had already discovered she had a vacancy—

"No." Justin sounded surprised. "What kind of phone call are you expecting?"

"Oh, never mind!" Disappointed, Jessica banged the door to her locker again. Gloomily she walked to the front of the locker room. Even under her heavy clothes, she could still smell the uniform. She imagined Lila in the air-conditioned dress shop at the mall, trying on furs, dealing with fancy, important people—

Well, this is it, she promised herself as she emerged from the locker room, blinking in the sunlight. *No matter what, this is my last day. Even if Mrs. Fiske doesn't come through. I'll find something else this afternoon. Anything else.*

Jessica narrowed her eyes as she walked toward where Justin was waiting for her.

I will never *shovel bear poop!*

*   *   *

"Just sit tight, and they'll get used to you," Madeleine advised Elizabeth. They'd just gone into the monkey cage together for the first time.

"Can I touch them?" Elizabeth half-whispered, longing to reach out and stroke their thick fur and long curly tails. She could see Spanky, the little gray one, staring curiously at her from the top of a branch. Nearby two other monkeys played raucously with a tennis ball.

Madeleine smiled. "I think they'll be wanting to touch you. Look, here comes Mr. Magoo."

A brown monkey who looked exactly like most of the others came forward, wobbling as he walked. He stared at Elizabeth for a moment. "Hello," Elizabeth said, leaning forward with a smile.

Mr. Magoo made a chattering noise and opened his mouth very wide. Elizabeth could see a red tongue and sharp little teeth.

"Oh, he's great!" Elizabeth said with enthusiasm. Before she knew it, Mr. Magoo had hopped into her lap. She gasped with surprise.

"He likes you," Madeleine said, grinning. Mr. Magoo whined a couple of times, then turned around the way a cat would, flicking his tail as he went.

This is incredibly awesome, Elizabeth thought. *Wait till I tell Amy and Maria about holding a monkey in my lap!*

Elizabeth reached out to stroke that silky fur. But she'd barely moved her hand when Mr. Magoo's body jerked. With a sudden shriek, he jumped down and ran, wobbling, toward a tree.

"Always reach from underneath," Madeleine advised her. "He thought you might be trying to hit him. They're so smart that way," she added, staring fondly after Mr. Magoo as he ran. "They're always thinking."

Elizabeth frowned. *What was so smart about that?* she thought to herself. *Isn't that just instinct—like the way people run away from loud noises?*

"Spanky seems to be enjoying himself," Madeleine noted, pointing to a tree behind Elizabeth.

Elizabeth turned. Spanky was chattering, staring right into her eyes. He almost looked as if he were laughing about the way Mr. Magoo had come and gone, she thought.

But that couldn't be, Elizabeth assured herself, grinning back at the little gray monkey.

Monkeys aren't smart enough to have a sense of humor!

"This is going to be so cool!"

Justin put his arm around Jessica. Jessica shrank back; Justin already smelled like he'd spent the night with the bears. "Even *you're* going to love this," Justin went on, scarcely noticing Jessica's resistance. "I'm so psyched, I can hardly think straight."

"What is it?" Jessica asked, curling her upper lip as Justin excitedly steered her toward the bear habitat. "Someone's invented bear perfume so they don't stink all day?"

"Better." Justin beamed. "The wildlife people just called. They have a mother grizzly bear and a cub that someone found outside a mall near Fresno!"

Thrills, chills, and excitement, Jessica thought, pretending to yawn. "Did the mall have a Briana Taylor clothing store?" she wanted to know.

Justin grinned. "Somehow I doubt they were after clothes," he said. "More likely the dumpster. Or one of those places where they sell cinnamon rolls."

Cinnamon rolls. Jessica shut her eyes and imagined the Sweet Valley Mall. Even with the bears all around, she could almost smell that wonderful scent.

"Anyway," Justin went on, talking a little faster, "the wildlife people shot them with a tranquilizer gun. That was just a couple of hours ago. They should sleep for another few hours."

"So what does this have to do with us?" Jessica asked haughtily. "I mean, they're not going to bring them to Sweet Valley, are they? It's not like they need bears at the Sweet Valley Mall."

"No," Justin agreed. "But they need a place to keep the mother and the baby till they can return them to the wild. And they've chosen the Sweet Valley Zoo for the next week or so." He stopped in front of an empty cage. "See that, Jessica?" he asked, clapping her on the back. "That's the future temporary home of Mama Grizzly and Grizzly T. Cub!"

Jessica thought she understood now. Some

dumb bears had been walking around a mall, so they got shot. *Lucky for them it was only a tranquilizer dart*, she said to herself. *They should have used a real gun. Bears ought to know better than that.* "If I saw a bear at the mall, I'd probably freak," she said aloud.

"Uh-huh." Justin wrinkled his nose. "Most people would. I never could figure that out."

"Figures," Jessica muttered under her breath.

"So the bears are coming here this afternoon," Justin went on, brightening again. "And that means we've got a ton of stuff to do. I've got to alert the newspapers," he said, checking his watch. "And there are other arrangements I'll have to make, too."

Jessica bit her lip. It sounded like Justin was going to monopolize the phone all morning. *Just who does he think he is, anyway?* she wondered.

Justin smiled. "But I can't do everything. For instance, someone needs to hose down the cage for the new arrivals, and I can't possibly get to it. It's at the end of the long hallway. Thanks so much for volunteering."

"Volunteering?" Jessica stared at Justin in astonishment.

Justin winked. "Of course, you could feed the brown bears if you'd rather. They're pretty hungry," he added carelessly. "But it's your choice."

Sheesh. "All right," Jessica muttered. "I'll hose it down. But I'm telling you, Justin, you're lucky I don't—" She broke off quickly.

"Don't what?" Justin asked with a grin.

Dozens of possibilities passed through Jessica's mind: dropping Justin off a cliff, feeding him to the lions, locking him in a room with Steven for three days. *I'll tell him when I'm out of here*, she thought furiously.

"Oh—forget it," she snarled, reaching for the hose.

"They're here!"

Justin ran into the bear habitat, practically jumping for joy. "You did a great job, Jessica," he said, pumping her hand. "Now if you'll stand back, we'll load 'em in."

A great job, huh? Jessica thought bitterly, smelling the sleeve of her sweater. *This smell will never come off. Even if I took a bath in tomato juice, I couldn't get rid of it.*

"Here they come!" Justin said happily. Jessica watched as the two bears were trucked down the corridor and laid gently on the floor of the cage, next to an old tree stump. *Bo-ring.*

"It's even better than TV, isn't it?" Justin turned his shining face toward her and grinned.

"Are you out of your mind?" Jessica snapped, wondering what soap operas she was missing. *Instead of* Days of Turmoil, she thought angrily, *I get* Days of Bear-moil. *Some great trade.*

The ranger from the wildlife department studied the sleeping bears. "We'd guess about another two hours or so till they wake up. The big one, anyway. The cub may be a little quicker."

Justin grabbed a pad of paper and scrawled a

few words on it. "Okay. Mind telling me how old you think the baby is?"

The ranger shrugged. "Can't be more than a week or two," he said, turning to go. "Okay, then. We'll be in touch."

When the ranger had left, Justin grabbed the key to the cage and locked it securely. "We don't want to take any chances," he said. "Sometimes they can get pretty mad when they wake up—especially since no one seems to know for sure how much tranquilizer the mother got."

Yeah, whatever, Jessica wanted to say. "Can I go back to the office now?" she asked instead.

Justin scratched his head. "Actually, Jessica, I need you for a little while longer. I have another meeting, and someone needs to watch these two bears until I get back."

Jessica opened her eyes as wide as she could. "You're kidding!" she said. "You want to put me—in there—with *them*?"

"Oh, no!" Justin looked shocked. "No, I just want you to watch them from out here. In fact—" He waved a forefinger in front of Jessica's face. "You're forbidden to even *touch* that key. Your safety's important, believe me."

Oh, sure it is, Jessica said to herself.

"OK, then," Justin said cheerfully. "I'll be over at the children's zoo if you need me."

Well. Jessica scowled, but at least she had to admit it wasn't as bad as hosing down the cage. "Just come back quickly, OK?"

"OK," Justin promised.

*   *   *

That was just the longest half hour of my life, Jessica thought a little later. From her chair in the long hallway outside the grizzlies' cage, she watched the mother's chest rising and falling, rising and falling. To pass the time, she was guessing how many minutes had gone by each time the bear changed position.

Maybe it wasn't only half an hour, she told herself hopefully. *Maybe it was really forty minutes. Forty-five, even—*

She checked her watch. *Only fifteen!* she thought with disgust. "Fifteen minutes," she said aloud, "and these stupid bears don't even *do* anything."

Actually, she could hardly see the little one from where she sat. And the mother did pretty much nothing but breathe.

All at once Jessica decided she couldn't stand it any longer. *No one's around*, she told herself. *It's a perfect time to go call Mrs. Fiske again. After all, she didn't say definitely no.*

But you promised to stay and watch the bears, a little voice in her head told her.

Jessica glanced up and down the rows of cages. *But there's no one else around*, she argued. *So who's to know?*

Jessica stood up before she could change her mind. "Hasta la vista, babies!" she called to the sleeping grizzlies in front of her. "I'll be right back!"

With quick steps she headed for the office.

How come Mrs. Fiske is never around when I need

her? Jessica thought angrily a few minutes later as she walked from the office back to the grizzlies' cage. Apparently, Mrs. Fiske spent Tuesdays out of the mall, doing makeovers at people's houses. Jessica had left her name and home phone number, just in case.

"Back to the dull and boring bears," she said aloud, wondering why it was that she always had such bad luck. She walked a little faster. *Not that I'm feeling guilty about leaving them,* she assured herself. *I'm just—well, in a hurry, OK?*

What was it Justin had called the bears: Mama Grizzly and Baby T. Grizzly? Something dumb, anyway, something that sounded like it was out of a silly kids' book. *I could name the bears myself,* Jessica thought, interested despite herself. *But I'd name them something really fashionable. Like "Mallory." Or "Monique." Yeah. Cool names like those.*

Rounding the corner, Jessica saw with relief that the hallway near the grizzly cage was still empty.

But as she stared out at the bears, she realized that something was very wrong.

Six

◇

Jessica drew in her breath sharply. "Oh, man," she said aloud, her words echoing through the empty halls of the bear habitat.

The mother bear was jerking and thrashing in her sleep. As Jessica watched nervously, the mother groaned and turned from her back to her side—to her back—to her side. Her breath was coming in great shuddering heaves. Jessica could hear the rasping noise the mother grizzly made with each breath. It sounded a little like a chainsaw.

Not quite as loud, maybe.

But more ominous.

Jessica backed away from the cage. *Maybe she's about to wake up,* she thought, licking her lips as the bear's left front paw twitched violently.

The bear's body spun around suddenly, like an enormous puppet on the end of a very long string.

Jessica could see little flecks of saliva around the mother grizzly's mouth.

Find Justin, her brain commanded. But her feet wouldn't budge. Jessica stood stock-still, staring out at the writhing mother bear. Beyond her she could dimly make out the outlines of the baby. As far as she could tell, he was sleeping peacefully.

The mother bear opened her mouth and gave a ghastly howl, though her eyes remained closed. Jessica felt the sound rip right through her. In a flash she was out the door, heading as fast as she could for—

For where?

To her horror, Jessica realized she'd forgotten where Justin had said he was going.

Yanking open the door to the main office, Jessica pulled herself to a stop in front of the secretary's desk. "Is Justin Marx here?" she asked breathlessly. She'd run all the way, and her chest felt as if it were on fire.

"I beg your pardon?" The secretary stared back at her quizzically.

"Justin Marx," Jessica said, her breath coming in gasps that reminded her alarmingly of the mother bear's. She forced herself to take a mouthful of air. "It's an emergency. Is Justin here?"

The secretary frowned. "Are you with the zoo?"

"I'm an intern!" Jessica grabbed the edge of the desk. "Please, please," she begged. "It's really important—"

"If you're with the zoo, where's your uniform?" the secretary asked suspiciously.

My uniform. Jessica gulped, suddenly remembering how she'd hidden it beneath the layers of clothes she'd brought from home. Frantically she clawed at the collar. "Under here. See?" she asked. She'd never thought she'd be so glad to see that flash of disgusting green.

"Well, I don't know why you'd cover it up," the secretary said in a disagreeable voice. She turned back to her work. "No, Justin's not here. I don't know where he is."

"How about Mrs.—" Jessica began. For the life of her, she couldn't remember the head zookeeper's name. "You know. The woman who's in charge?"

"Mrs. Tomlinson," the woman replied acidly. "No, she's out of the office, at a meeting downtown."

Fine. Just fine. "Well, if you see Justin," Jessica began, turning for the door, "would you tell him I need him? Like, right now?"

Without waiting for an answer, she was out the door and running toward the parking lot.

Justin's car was easy to find: a Jeep, plastered with bear bumper stickers and a license plate that read BEAR IT. *Well, he hasn't left the zoo, anyway,* Jessica thought gratefully. *But—where is he?*

She strained to think. What parts of the zoo had she heard people talk about? "Elizabeth's with the monkeys, I know that for sure," she muttered, checking one of the signposts that pointed to some of the zoo's attractions. "The birds—that's Bruce, I remember that." She frowned. The children's zoo sounded familiar, too—as if someone had mentioned it not so long ago. *Well, that must have been Melissa, then,* Jessica figured.

She looked at her watch. Fifteen minutes already!

No doubt about it, Jessica thought as she dashed back to the bear habitat. It was the quickest fifteen minutes she'd ever spent in her life.

"Justin?"

Jessica dashed into the building and down the long hall, hoping against hope that he would be there. But there was no sign of him.

She pressed her face up against the grizzly cage. *Thank goodness,* she thought, feeling her entire body relax as she saw that the mother bear was no longer kicking. *She must have been having a nightmare, or something,* Jessica assured herself.

"You sure scared me," she said aloud, wiping her forehead with the back of her hand. "No more jerking around, OK, Mrs. Monique Bear?" She wiggled her finger, pretending to scold the big grizzly. "We'll make a rule against practically crushing your little baby under your paws, all right? No more loud noises, either." Despite herself, she grinned down at the huge bear lying as still as could be in front of her.

Wait a minute.

Jessica leaned forward and frowned. Something was wrong. The bear was almost *too* calm.

Jessica held her breath and bent down so her eyes were level with the top of the mother's chest.

She looked for the old familiar rising and falling of the chest.

But there was none.

She isn't moving! Jessica thought, a sense of panic rising in her. *She isn't breathing! She's—*

"No, she can't be," Jessica said aloud. Her throat felt dry.

There was only one thing to do. Jessica grabbed the key from the rack—the key she'd been forbidden to touch.

Her hand trembled as she tried to insert the key in the lock.

Move, Jessica begged the mother bear with every ounce of energy she had. *Just do something to show you're not—you know. Sit up, roll over, anything!*

The door swung gently open. The bear lay motionless.

Jessica took a tentative step into the cage. *She can't be dead—can she?*

Heart beating furiously, Jessica inched closer and closer to the mother grizzly. "Please, let it be alive," she begged aloud. Then she had an even more alarming thought.

What if it's only playing dead? What if this is just a trap to get me close so it can bite my head off?

But as Jessica came nearer, she could see that the bear couldn't be playing dead. A bear pretending to be dead wouldn't hold its head at such a strange angle. No living bear could possibly lie so terrifyingly still. Setting her jaw so tight she thought her teeth might crack, Jessica leaned over the mother bear's face.

Oh, man, she thought hollowly, as she saw the silent face, the expressionless eyes, the paws that would never cuddle a baby bear again—

The baby bear. Jessica gasped. Suddenly, beyond the mother bear's body appeared the saddest pair of big brown eyes that Jessica had ever seen. The cub blinked once—twice. And then, as Jessica watched, hardly daring to breathe, the cub began to moan.

Jessica didn't think twice. Reaching for the motherless baby, she picked him up and held him close against her. He was surprisingly light. The cub moaned again and snuggled right in. He seemed to fit perfectly between her shoulder and her neck.

"Good boy." Jessica spoke to him softly as she stroked the warm, furry body. She could feel the cub relax. "Good boy. Everything's going to be OK."

The cub stretched its legs and cuddled in closer.

Jessica slowly sat down on the tree stump, pressing the cub tightly against her chest. She could feel its tiny heart racing. "Of course," she murmured. "You've had quite a shock, poor little guy. One minute you're looking for lunch in Fresno, and the next—" She bit her lip.

The next minute, you wake up in a zoo, and your mother's—dead.

Stroking the deep, smooth fur of the little cub, she looked down at the mother again. Tears welled up in her eyes. *It isn't fair,* she thought for about the third time in the last two days. *It just isn't fair!*

But this time, she realized as she blinked back the tears, she was worrying about the baby bear—and not about herself.

Jessica felt hands touching her shoulder. She spun around to see Justin standing behind her. How long had she been sitting here?

"Are you OK?" Justin's face seemed somehow pinched.

Jessica nodded numbly. The baby bear was asleep again, pressed cozily against her chest. "But—the mother—" she began, leaning forward so as not to waken the cub. "I—"

"It's all right." Justin's tone was gentle, but he was shaking his head. "We'll figure it out. Here, give me this little guy for a minute."

Justin reached down for the cub, and Jessica relaxed her grip. Instantly the bear awoke and dug its claws deep into her sweater. With a whine, it tried to burrow back into her arms.

"Go with Justin," Jessica told the cub, afraid she might be about to cry again. She breathed deeply and swallowed. Circling her hands around the baby's back legs, she tried to unhook him from her sweater.

The bear whimpered and kicked. His head nuzzled against Jessica's neck and then lay still.

"Well." Justin blinked down at the baby. He stood back and frowned. "It looks like he just wants you, Jessica. Um—he'll be hungry soon, though. Would you mind—?" He motioned to a nearby box with some emergency supplies.

Jessica blushed with satisfaction. "Well—all right."

"Good." Justin smiled. "I'll fill a bottle with some warm milk for him. Be right back."

"OK," Jessica said dreamily, not taking her eyes off the beautiful creature in front of her.

She stroked its fur as it lay snuggled in her arms. For a moment she remembered how yesterday she'd imagined herself modeling fur coats at the mall. She'd been thrilled with the idea. But today, well . . .

Funny how she'd never noticed just how amazing fur was when it was attached to a baby bear!

Seven

"It's quarter to six," Justin told Jessica, bending toward her. "Almost time for the zoo to close."

"Oh." With a start, Jessica looked up. She had been so involved in holding the little baby bear, she'd completely lost track of the time. They were sitting in the bear-habitat office, where Jessica and the cub had gone while the body of the mother bear had been taken away. "Do I have to—you know—leave now?"

Justin nodded. "I'm afraid so."

Jessica sighed deeply, looking down at the baby bear. He looked up at her with watery brown eyes, and she rocked him gently back and forth. *Poor little guy . . .*

Justin squatted lower and rested his hand on Jessica's shoulder. "Jessica," he said, even more gently than before. "How do you feel?"

"Oh—fine," Jessica said, not daring to meet

Justin's eyes. "Fine. Just fine." The awful image of the mother bear crept into her mind—the bear thrashing violently back and forth on the floor of its cage. She shuddered.

"Jessica." Now Justin's voice was firm. "This has been a shock to you, hasn't it? Be honest, now."

Jessica gulped and held the bear tighter to her body. "I said, I'm fine!" A prickle of guilt crept up her spine. *What if*—she thought, swallowing hard. *What if I hadn't gone to make that phone call? What if I'd remembered where Justin was?* She shook her head hard, trying to brush the thoughts away. "I'm just fine," she repeated, her fingers quickly stroking the baby bear's fur.

Justin sat with her a moment longer, then stood and began to pace around the office. "I feel pretty wrung out about all this myself, but maybe you're different from me that way. I know bears aren't your favorite things in the world." He grinned slightly; then he turned serious again. "But it's always hard when an animal dies."

"Uh-huh," Jessica said, not trusting herself to say anything more. She tried hard not to think of the mother bear lying motionless on the ground. Gently she ruffled the fur of the cub in her arms.

Justin squatted again. "But there's one thing you shouldn't do, Jessica, and that's blame yourself. You did what you could." He sighed. "The mother died because they shot too much tranquilizer into her, that's all there is to it. She couldn't have been saved, no matter what."

Tears welled up in Jessica's eyes. She could no

longer keep the question from forming on her lips. "But what if I'd noticed first thing?" she asked, straining hard to keep from sobbing. "What if I'd— you know, found you right away and then—" Her face began to collapse. *Then this little bear wouldn't have had to lose his mother,* she thought miserably.

Justin smiled softly. "Jessica," he said, "haven't you been listening to anything I've been saying?" He shook his head. "It isn't your fault. It doesn't matter what you did—or what you didn't do," he added quickly, looking meaningfully at Jessica. "The bear was doomed the moment the tranquilizer dart hit her skin."

"But—" Jessica began once more, fresh tears trickling down her cheeks.

"But nothing." Justin straightened up. "You were a real hero, Jessica, whether you want to believe it or not. It must have been terrifying to walk into that cage, not knowing if the mother was dead or alive. And to help out that little orphan cub when he needed a little loving—" He cleared his throat. "Well, it took some guts."

Little orphan cub, Jessica repeated to herself. She couldn't stand it any more. Burying her head in the cub's soft fur, she started to cry loudly.

In the distance Jessica could hear a bell chiming. *Six o'clock,* she thought, drying her eyes as best she could in the bathroom of the bear-habitat office. She decided not to look at her reflection in the mirror.

I hope the little bear will be all right here overnight

without me, she thought guiltily as she pushed the door open. She'd heard him whimpering almost the whole time she'd been in the bathroom. *What if he cries? What if he—*

The bear cub caught sight of her as she stepped into the office. Immediately he tried to wiggle out of Justin's arms and reach for her.

"Oh—" Jessica practically melted. Backing away slowly, she tried hard to keep her arms at her sides.

"She'll see you tomorrow," Justin promised. The cub seemed to relax a little, and Justin smiled. "You really should give this cub a name," he said to Jessica.

"Me?" Jessica asked with surprise.

Justin nodded. "He certainly seems to like you best."

Names began to flash through Jessica's head. *Shane—Scott—*She frowned. *Something macho. Something trendy. Brett? Travis? Maybe Ross?*

Then it hit her. "His name is Gus."

"Gus, huh?" Justin stared at the bear in his arms, then looked at Jessica, the trace of a smile playing around his face. "Funny. I'd have guessed you'd choose something like, I don't know, Rick, Forrest, something like that. Something kind of strong and cool sounding."

"Oh, yeah?" Jessica decided not to admit that Gus was the name of her old teddy bear. She tossed her hair. "Well, I happen to think the name Gus sounds pretty cool."

"OK." Justin nodded slowly. "He looks like a Gus, at that," he agreed, examining the bear closely.

"Good choice, Jessica. Now I'm afraid you're really going to have to go."

Jessica bit her lip. "Good-bye, Gus," she whispered, bending low and giving the little bear a kiss on the forehead. He kicked and gurgled—but as Jessica headed for the door, the gurgle turned into a long drawn-out cry.

Jessica walked stiffly to her bike, sending Gus a silent, urgent message that she desperately hoped he understood. *It's OK, Gus. I'll be back really, really soon.*

"I don't understand it," Elizabeth said at the dinner table that night. "Madeleine keeps saying that the monkeys are so smart, but I just don't see it."

Steven grinned. "You know what?" he asked in a high-pitched chattering voice. "Madeleine keeps saying that that girl who works in our cage is so smart, and I just don't see it!" He'd heard enough about monkeys and their habits for one day. Couldn't they talk about something else for a change?

"Knock it off, Steven," Mrs. Wakefield said wearily.

"I mean, they're lots of fun and all that," Elizabeth went on, paying no attention to her brother, "but all they do is sit around and pick nits off each other. I just don't think that's exactly intelligent."

"Oh?" Steven asked. "And would it be more intelligent to *not* pick the nits off each other?"

Elizabeth sighed. "That's not what I mean, Steven."

Steven grinned. "I thought it was a good question."

Elizabeth turned back toward her parents, ignoring him. "Know what Spanky did today?" she asked, dipping a spoon into her bowl of soup.

Steven glowered at his plate. How come Elizabeth was so tough to tease sometimes? He turned to his left, figuring that Jessica would be a better target. "Hey, Jess," he hissed. "I hear you get some *really cute* uniforms when you work at the zoo. Tell me about it, huh?"

"Hmm," Jessica replied dreamily, munching her salad.

"Earth to Jessica!" he chanted, waving his hand in front of Jessica's face. "Come in, Jessica!"

"Shh!" Mr. Wakefield pointed toward Elizabeth, who was still talking about Spanky.

Steven sank back innocently in his chair. "Who, me?" he mumbled. "I wasn't talking. Hey, I barely said—"

"What's that?" Jessica suddenly leaned forward, her eyes shining. "What did you say?"

"Huh?" Steven made a face. "I didn't say anything. Just that—just that I didn't say anything."

"Oh." Jessica was clearly disappointed. "I thought you were talking about bears."

Bears? Steven frowned, trying to remember what he'd said. *Who, me? I wasn't talking,* he repeated in his mind. *Hey, I barely—*

Barely. Bear-ly. For Pete's sake!

Grimacing at his plate, he started to attack his own salad.

Sisters!

*   *   *

Jessica smiled to herself, remembering the way Gus's long silky fur had felt against her shoulder. It was nearly bedtime, and she'd scarcely thought about anything else since she'd arrived home. She'd even asked her parents if they wanted a "cub of tea." Jessica giggled. No doubt about it, she had bears on the brain!

She had brushed her teeth and was about to get under the covers when a thought struck her. Crossing the room to her closet, she dug carefully under the pile of stuff until she found what she was looking for.

The original Gus.

He was awfully threadbare in places, and one eye was hanging by a single string. *But he's soft,* she thought, *and he's the next best thing to the real Gus.*

Turning out the light, she nestled Gus up against her shoulder. It felt almost as nice as it had this afternoon. Rocking gently back and forth, she stroked his warm soft fur until she began to feel drowsy. Then, feeling the pressure of his face against her cheek, she curled up and drifted off to sleep.

Eight

◇

"Jessica!" Mrs. Wakefield's voice floated upstairs the next morning. "Awake yet, sweetie? There's a phone call for you."

A phone call? Jessica was usually a zombie in the morning, but the idea of a phone call made her snap wide awake. "I'll be right there, Mom!" she promised.

As she hopped out of bed, her old stuffed bear plunged to the floor and lay on his face. Jessica didn't bother to pick him up. *Weird,* she thought. She had only the vaguest memory of having taken Gus out at all last night. Still in her nightgown, she rushed downstairs.

"Hello?" she said into the phone.

"Hi, Jessica." It was Lila. "Just calling to ask about how your internship is going."

Jessica shook her head to remove the last few cobwebs. *My internship. The zoo,* she thought to herself.

There was that cute little bear cub—Yesterday seemed awfully far away, but she smiled as she remembered the cub burrowing into her arms. "What about my internship?" she asked.

Lila laughed. "Well, I'm having the time of my life at Briana Taylor's," she said meaningfully. "Yesterday, you know, I got to model these incredibly slinky dresses."

"Model them?" Jessica repeated, her stomach feeling hollow with envy.

"You got it!" Lila paused. "Well, not model them, exactly, but I was packing them from one box to another and—"

"You got to *touch* a box of slinky dresses?" Jessica fingered the soft material of the nightgown she was wearing. Her own internship was coming back to her, little by little. Suddenly the coveralls she'd been wearing at the zoo seemed even more ridiculous than they had before.

"That's right." Lila chuckled. "So I heard where *your* internship is, Jessica," she said. "I heard you were working at the—" She giggled. "Zoo."

"So?" Jessica barked into the mouthpiece.

"So nothing." Lila chuckled again. "And then there were the fur coats—"

"Fur coats?" Jessica couldn't help herself. "You got to *touch* them?"

"Hmm? Oh, wow, it's late," Lila said lightly. "I have to get to work. I hope you're having a really radical time, Jess. I know *I* am!" With a click, Lila hung up.

"Well, of all the nerve!" Jessica banged down the

phone in disgust. *It's bad enough to have to wear those stupid coveralls*, she thought bleakly. *And now Lila has to find out about it!*

Suddenly Jessica's time with the bear cub yesterday not only seemed long ago, it seemed downright silly. Bear fur was nothing compared with beautiful silky mink or fox coats. Now that Jessica thought about it, she could remember plenty of bumpy places on Gus's coat, places where tufts of fur stuck together in a kind of dirty way. Not exactly as nice as a real fur coat.

It wasn't fair. *Here I am making a fool of myself over a stupid bear*, Jessica thought as she stomped upstairs to change. *And there's Lila, practically modeling unbelievably gorgeous dresses—*

The phone rang again. "Don't answer it!" Jessica yelled. "It's probably another one of my so-called friends!"

"Hello?" Mrs. Wakefield picked up the receiver. Despite herself, Jessica stood on the stairway and listened. "Sure, one moment, please," Mrs. Wakefield went on. "Who's calling?" She listened for a moment, then motioned to Jessica. "It's for you," she hissed. "A Mrs. Sisk, or something like that."

Jessica's heart skipped. *Mrs. Fiske!*

"Jessica Wakefield here," Jessica said in her most grown-up voice.

"Jessica." Mrs. Fiske sounded tired. "Mrs. Fiske from Sweet Valley Makeovers. You'd called about a possible internship opening."

"Yes?" Jessica replied breathlessly.

"One of our employees has just left us," Mrs. Fiske went on sourly, "so we do have an opening after all. If you're still interested—"

"Oh, yes!" Jessica wondered if she was coming on too strong. "That is, I believe so," she corrected herself. "Um—when would you like me to start?"

"This morning, if possible." Mrs. Fiske sighed. "I do hate to replace paid labor with unpaid, but desperate times call for desperate measures."

Jessica thought that was probably an insult, but she decided she was too happy to care. "I'll be right over, Mrs. Fiske," she said joyfully, and hung up before Mrs. Fiske could change her mind.

"Hey, Elizabeth!" she called, bounding into the kitchen where Elizabeth was eating a bowl of cereal. "Do me a favor, OK? Tell Justin Marx I won't be coming back."

"You—what?" Elizabeth stared at her sister in surprise. "But—why?"

Jessica put her hands on her hips. "You're looking at the new trainee at Sweet Valley Makeovers! So will you tell Justin, please?" She reached for the phone.

"I—I guess so," Elizabeth agreed with a frown. "You know, you should call the school, too. Lots of people wanted the zoo internship, and if you're going to drop it—"

"Later," Jessica said breezily. She couldn't be bothered by those details just now.

She was too busy dialing Lila's number.

Bruce took a deep breath and walked out of the

locker room, pants neatly rolled up above his shoes. *Time to enter the crypt,* he thought, staring glumly at the aviary ahead of him. *Time to walk into the jaws of death. The chamber of horrors. The—*

"Time to go, Bruce." Melissa poked him. Bruce jumped.

"Oh, yeah. Sure," he said confidently, leading the way to the aviary. He was actually doing pretty well, he thought. Considering. On Tuesday, he hadn't screamed once.

Not out loud, anyway.

"Aren't you just having the best time, Bruce?" Melissa asked as they walked along the path.

Bruce cleared his throat. "Oh, yeah. The best."

"I just can't get over how beautiful they all are," Melissa went on. "The way their feathers shimmer in the sun, the way their wings spread when they glide through the air—it's gorgeous."

"Gorgeous," Bruce repeated hollowly. It wasn't exactly the word he would have chosen.

Melissa pulled open the aviary gate. "I mean, look at that one." She pointed to the top of the aviary. Bruce followed her gaze. An enormous bird with the sharpest claws Bruce had ever seen had just pushed off the narrow beam on top of the pole. Down it came, wings spread wide, closer and closer and closer—

"Look out!" Bruce cried, the words catching in his throat. *This is it!* he thought frantically as he dived to the dirt and covered his head.

There was silence.

"Bruce?" Melissa sounded concerned.

Suddenly, Bruce realized he'd protected himself but had forgotten to protect Melissa. He looked up. Melissa was standing there, a funny expression on her face. And the hawk was nowhere to be seen.

Oops. Scrambling to his feet, Bruce brushed off his uniform. "Um—I tripped," he explained suavely.

Melissa looked at him doubtfully.

"That's right." Bruce flashed her what he hoped was a cool-looking grin. Normally, he didn't especially want to come across as someone who tripped all over himself, but under the circumstances. . . . "Yup, just tripped, that's all."

Nine

"Jessica! Get to work!"

"Right away, Mrs. Fiske," Jessica said, dashing into the storeroom for another case of mascara.

It was only eleven o'clock, but Jessica already felt as if she'd put in a full day's work. Panting, she grabbed the case of mascara and hustled back. "The phone's ringing," Mrs. Fiske snapped. "Answer it!"

"Yes, ma'am." Jessica resisted the urge to salute. "Sweet Valley Makeovers!" she said into the receiver.

"I need an appointment right away." The voice at the other end of the line was firm.

"Um—yes, ma'am," Jessica said, anxiously looking over her shoulder at Mrs. Fiske, who was applying mascara to a customer's lashes. "One moment, please." Cupping her hand over the mouthpiece, she made frantic gestures at Mrs. Fiske.

"What's the problem?" Mrs. Fiske looked up.

"A customer," Jessica hissed. "She wants an appointment."

"Put her on hold," Mrs. Fiske said. "I'll be there in a minute."

"Will you hold, please?" Jessica asked into the phone. Without waiting for an answer, she pressed the proper button on the console.

Sighing deeply, Jessica sank into a chair and looked around the small store. *I should be enjoying myself*, she thought. *Lipstick. Blush. Rouge. Tan Number One and Rose Number Two.* Even the air smelled wonderfully fragrant. But for some reason she couldn't quite figure out, Jessica wasn't happy.

"Jessica!" Mrs. Fiske called sharply.

Jessica hopped up with a start. "Coming!" she gasped.

Well, I'll get used to it, she told herself, hoping she was right.

"See, look at the way they groom each other's fur," Madeleine said softly, pointing at a cluster of monkeys behind a tree. "It looks like a free-for-all, but it's not. Monkeys have very important rules about who grooms who and when."

"Really?" Elizabeth asked with a frown. She examined the monkeys carefully. It certainly *looked* like a free-for-all to her.

"Absolutely." Madeleine waved her hand toward the monkeys. "See, Howler is the leader of this pack. Capuchin will groom him, but not the other way around. The more powerful you are, the more other monkeys will groom you. Now watch. Here comes Bullwinkle." She pointed to a scruffy-looking monkey on the edge of the group. "He's at the bottom of the heap. In a moment, he'll start grooming someone—maybe Screeches, or Miss Milwaukee. But no one will groom *him*."

Elizabeth kept watching. Bullwinkle took a few tentative steps toward the pack. Three big brown monkeys were using their fingers to comb through the hair of another big brown monkey—Howler, Elizabeth realized. Now that Elizabeth knew what to look for, she saw that Howler did look sleeker and better cared for than the rest of the monkeys. Bullwinkle approached them and sat down. The others chattered and looked away.

"Poor thing," Elizabeth murmured. Bullwinkle looked like he could use some cleaning.

"It's OK," Madeleine replied. "He knows where he fits in. Wait and see."

Bullwinkle reached out slowly toward one of the groomers. With surprising gentleness, he dug a finger into the other one's back and began to pick his way through the fur.

"Their whole social system is very sophisticated," Madeleine continued. "It's one of the ways we know monkeys are so smart."

Elizabeth tried hard to understand what Madeleine was talking about. But she just couldn't see it.

Smart? she thought, shaking her head. *Sophisticated?*

The monkeys *were* incredibly cute, but the way they refused to groom Bullwinkle seemed to her a little mean. *Actually,* Elizabeth thought, *it's kind of how the Unicorns treat people, including each other.* And even though Elizabeth loved her sister, she would never call Jessica's Unicorn friends especially intelligent.

"Jessica!"

Jessica started. Mrs. Fiske was staring daggers at her.

"I asked for a box of brown eyebrow pencils," Mrs. Fiske snapped. "And here you bring me black!" She held out the box to Jessica. "Please fix your mistake."

"I'm—I'm sorry," Jessica said unhappily.

Mrs. Fiske glared over the top of her glasses. "See that it doesn't happen again."

Jessica darted back to the storeroom and found the right box almost at once. She was about to head back out when she realized that the pencils were an awfully familiar color.

Gus, she thought wildly. She took another look. No question about it—the pencils matched the shade of the little bear's fur. A memory flashed into her mind—a memory that was somehow clearer and more vivid than it was this morning: Gus nuzzled against her at the zoo, Gus crying when she left, Gus holding his little paws out to her—

Gus. Jessica held on to the memory. Gus's fur seemed almost real enough to ruffle.

"Jessica!" Mrs. Fiske sounded angry.

"Coming!" Jessica walked out to Mrs. Fiske, holding the Gus-colored pencils close to her chest.

*   *   *

"Well, if you're so smart, how come you never try to open your locked gate?" Elizabeth asked Spanky. He was still one of the few monkeys she could tell from the others.

Spanky smiled to reveal his white teeth. Then he pointed at Elizabeth and began to chatter.

Whatever that means! Elizabeth couldn't help laughing.

"Elizabeth?" Madeleine walked over. "Justin Marx from the bear habitat just called up. Could you go visit the bears for a little while? Sounds like it's important."

Elizabeth slipped off her chair. "Sure, Madeleine," she said with a smile. "I'd be happy to." She turned to Spanky. "Don't escape while I'm gone, now."

"Chee, chee!" Spanky chattered.

"Careful what you say," Madeleine cautioned her. "The monkeys are—"

Smarter than you think, Elizabeth finished silently, rolling her eyes.

"Smarter than you think!" Madeleine said with a grin.

"Good morning, ma'am," Jessica said to the well-dressed woman in front of her. "Are you here for a makeover?"

The woman looked at Jessica pointedly. "No, I'm here for a game of tennis."

"Oh." Jessica stared at the woman in confusion. "I think the nearest tennis courts are behind the gym at school."

The woman narrowed her eyes. "Of course I want a makeover. I've got an appointment with Mrs. Blair."

"With Mrs. Bear?" Jessica gasped, leaning eagerly forward. "Mrs.—oh." *Mrs. Blair,* she thought. *Mrs. Fiske's assistant.* She slumped back again. "OK. I'll tell her."

I wonder how Gus is doing, she said to herself as she signaled Mrs. Blair. *I hope he doesn't—*

She swallowed hard.

I hope he doesn't miss me too much.

"He's been whining all day long, and all night before that," Justin told Elizabeth, his voice full of exasperation. He pointed to the little bear lying in the corner, its big brown eyes damp and sad. "Of course, bears don't feel emotion exactly the way people do, but I'd almost swear he misses Jessica. He's been at it ever since your sister left."

Elizabeth went closer to the little bear. "He's really cute," she said.

"He is." Justin shook his head. "And nothing helps him. Not a bottle, not another bear, nothing. So we were wondering," he went on quickly, "since Jessica quit on us, maybe he'd respond to you." He scooped up the little bear cub. "I mean, you guys look exactly alike and all. How about it? Want to try?"

Elizabeth's heart leaped. This would be even better than the monkeys. "I'd love to," she told him.

Justin smiled. "I'd hoped you'd say that." He turned to the little bear. "Hey, Gus!" he said in a soothing voice. "Look who's here."

Gus turned his head gently to one side. When he caught sight of Elizabeth, he instantly stopped crying and began to wave his paws in the air. "Oh, he's adorable," Elizabeth said, proud that Gus wanted to be with her.

"What do you know?" Justin said heartily. "I knew it would work." He handed the cub to Elizabeth. Somewhat awkwardly, she tucked Gus against her chest.

Gus sighed deeply and began to curl up. Then suddenly his body stiffened.

"It's OK," Elizabeth crooned, stroking his fur.

But it was no use. With a sudden motion, Gus kicked and arched his back. He made a peculiar howling sound, louder than before. "Help," Elizabeth gasped, afraid of losing her grip.

"Son of a gun!" Justin said, hurrying forward to grab Gus's head before he toppled over. "She's a friend," he told Gus softly. "You'll be safe with her. Promise." He began to push Gus back into Elizabeth's arms.

Gus growled again and kicked hard, his foot banging into Elizabeth's wrist. "Oooh!" Elizabeth winced and let go of the bear cub.

"Come *on*, Gus," Justin pleaded. But no matter how hard he tried, he couldn't convince Gus to accept Elizabeth. At last Justin shook his head sorrowfully and tucked Gus, still growling, under his arm. "I guess it didn't work," he said. "Gus must be able to tell the difference between you two—somehow. Thanks for trying. I'm sorry."

"That's OK," Elizabeth said, turning to leave. *I'm sorry, too,* she thought as she walked back toward the monkey house. *It would have been kind of fun being mother to an orphan bear.*

She couldn't help feeling a little hurt. *How come he likes Jessica and not me?* she wondered, walking up the steps toward the monkey cage. Ahead of her she could see the monkeys leaping around, chattering and chattering and chattering—

"Smart, huh?" Elizabeth said to them, shaking her head.

"Bet *you* guys couldn't tell the difference between me and my sister!"

"Jessica!"

Jessica could hardly hear Mrs. Fiske's latest outburst. She was too busy in the back room, looking at all the bear-brown makeup that reminded her so much of Gus. *I hope he's all right,* she thought for about the fifteenth time. *I hope losing his mother won't scar him for life, and I hope he's getting used to Justin, and—*

"Jessica!"

Is Justin holding Gus with his paws out, the way he likes? Jessica asked herself, biting her lip.

"Jes-si-ca Wakefield!"

Jessica snapped to attention. "Yes, ma'am!"

Mrs. Fiske sighed loudly. "You have a telephone call. He says it's important."

Jessica hurried out of the back room, blinking in the light. "Important?" She picked up the phone. "Hello?"

"In the future," Mrs. Fiske snapped, "kindly tell your friends that you are not allowed to take personal calls while—"

"Jessica? It's Justin. Marx. From the zoo?"

Jessica's heart skipped a beat. "Yes?" she asked eagerly.

Justin sighed. "I'm—I'm sorry to bother you. I know you're happier doing makeovers, but I wanted to ask a personal favor."

"How's Gus doing?" Jessica broke in.

Mrs. Fiske snorted and turned toward the next customer.

"Actually, that's what I wanted to talk to you about," Justin said apologetically. "I was wondering if you could stop by the zoo this afternoon. He's just been impossible without you."

"He has?" Jessica practically melted in her seat. "Has he been crying a lot?"

"Buckets," Justin said wryly.

"Then I'll come right now," Jessica said quickly. Hanging up, she turned to her boss. "Mrs. Fiske, I'll need to take off a few minutes early today, OK?"

Mrs. Fiske looked at her frostily. "It's twenty minutes to three, Jessica. You want to leave *twenty* minutes early, so that you can see your *boyfriend?*"

Jessica gave Mrs. Fiske her sweetest smile. "Not exactly," she replied. "Not my boyfriend. A bear."

Mrs. Fiske blinked. "What are you—"

But Jessica was already racing out of the store.

"Oh, Gus," Jessica sighed happily. The moment

Justin had placed him in her arms, Gus had stopped crying. Now he was nestled snugly against her chest. "You're such a cutie pie."

"You two are amazing," Justin said. "He sure needed you, Jessica. Till now, he hadn't stopped crying all day."

"Well, I'm glad I could be here." Jessica offered the cub a bottle. Greedily he sucked at the nipple.

Justin paused. "How long can you stay?"

Jessica took a deep breath. She'd come to a decision on her way over here, and now that she actually had Gus in her arms, she was sure it was the right one. "Well—I was thinking," she said. "I mean, makeup's my career goal and everything, but since Gus really needs me. . . ." She let her words trail off carelessly.

A grin spread across Justin's face. "Really?" he asked. "You want to come back?"

"I guess so," Jessica said, trying to sound as unenthusiastic as possible. No need to let Justin see how eager she was.

"Well, what do you know?" Justin said, shaking his head. "I thought for sure you'd rather give makeovers than spend time with bears."

"Yeah, well," Jessica said dismissively, rubbing her cheek against Gus's sleek fur. "I decided that this shade of brown looks better on Gus than on an eyebrow pencil, that's all."

Ten

◇

"I don't know, Elizabeth," Melissa said early on Thursday morning. "Bruce is just plain acting weird."

The two girls were changing in the locker room before starting work. "What do you mean?" Elizabeth wanted to know, pulling up her coveralls.

Melissa sighed as she closed her locker. "Well, for one thing, he walks up to the birds totally terrified—it's like he thinks they're carrying guns or something."

Elizabeth laughed, imagining a little sparrow flying around with a rifle under its wing.

"And every time there's any kind of strange noise, he hits the deck," Melissa went on. "And you can see the muscles in the back of his neck tighten up whenever a big bird comes anywhere near."

"Big, tough Bruce afraid of birds?" Elizabeth's eyes danced at the idea.

"Well, he doesn't admit it or anything," Melissa said. "But it's easy to tell. He's always acting so stuck-up at school, it's kind of nice to see him so— so *worried* about something for a change."

"That *must* be something," Elizabeth said with a grin.

Melissa gazed wistfully into space. "You know, it's funny. I never thought much about him at school, because he's so arrogant and everything. But he's really kind of—" She blushed. "Well, kind of cute."

Elizabeth's eyes twinkled as she zipped her uniform. "That's what people say."

Melissa brushed off her own uniform. "Too bad he's so arrogant, though." She cleared her throat. "Anyway, enough about me. How are things going for you?"

Elizabeth shrugged. "OK, I guess. It's just that— well, the monkeys are beginning to get to me."

"Get to you how?" Melissa asked.

"Oh, nothing." Elizabeth made a face. "I mean, they're incredibly cute and lots of fun—but Madeleine keeps telling me how smart they are, and I just don't see it."

"Maybe she's overestimating them," Melissa suggested, pushing open the door.

"Could be," Elizabeth agreed. "I mean, they're just animals, after all."

"Yeah." Melissa grinned and turned left. "Well, have fun. Catch you later."

"You too," Elizabeth said. *They're just animals,* her brain repeated over and over as she walked off to the monkey house. *Just animals. And pretty dumb ones, too.*

She passed the crocodiles, sitting quietly and thoughtfully on the banks of their man-made river, waiting for their prey to come along. *Now those are smart animals*, Elizabeth thought. *No chattering. No jumping around. No picking bugs off each other.*

She rounded a corner and saw a lone lion gently swishing bugs with its tail. *And there's another smart one*, Elizabeth told herself, frowning as she compared the lion to her monkeys. *It stands all by itself so the rest of the lions can't fight with it and yell in its ear.* She nodded. *Now that's intelligence!*

The deer seemed pretty sharp, too, and so did the seals and even the warthogs. In fact, by the time Elizabeth reached the monkey house, she was convinced that monkeys were about the dumbest animals on earth.

Man's closest relative, Elizabeth thought sarcastically, carefully unlocking the door to the biggest cage.

Ha!

"So what's Spanky been up to today?" Madeleine asked Elizabeth just before three that afternoon.

"Chee, chee!" Spanky shouted from his perch on a tree.

Elizabeth grinned. "Oh, he's been up to everything, Madeleine." She thought back. "He's been taunting me from that tree almost all day. Earlier on, he wouldn't eat unless I was watching him—"

She smiled at the memory. "He's a pretty mischie-vous monkey, I guess."

"A very smart monkey," Madeleine corrected her. "Doesn't he remind you of some of the smartest people you know?"

Elizabeth blinked. "Well—not exactly," she said. "To tell you the truth, he reminds me mostly of some of the show-offy-est boys I know at school." *Like Bruce Patman*, she thought, rolling her eyes. *Or even better—*

"Chee, chee, chee!" Spanky shouted, flicking his tail wildly back and forth.

"Like my brother," Elizabeth said with a laugh. "Yeah, Steven would fit right in here, I think." She could just see him up on the tree next to Spanky, the two of them shaking their fists at zoo visitors and shouting "Chee, chee, chee!"

Madeleine shrugged. "Well, remember to lock the cage when you leave."

"Of course," Elizabeth told her as Madeleine disappeared into the monkey-house office.

Elizabeth checked her watch. Three o'clock. She wondered whether she should stop by the bear habitat and pick up Jessica. Then she remembered that Jessica planned to stay at the zoo till closing time so she could play with Gus.

"Well, I'll see you guys later," Elizabeth called out to the monkeys.

"Chee, chee, chee!" Spanky shrieked.

Elizabeth unlocked the door and walked through. She was just about to close the door when there was a commotion behind her.

"Chee, chee, chee!"

Elizabeth whirled around to see two of the big brown monkeys wrestling around on the floor. "Stop that!" she yelled loudly, taking a step toward them. "Stop it right now!" She waved her hands angrily around as she had seen Madeleine do when fights broke out. Which was often.

"Cut it out!" she bellowed, stepping even closer.

All at once the two monkeys separated and sat looking at her, innocent expressions on their faces.

There, Elizabeth thought, smiling with satisfaction. *I'm really getting the hang of this zookeeping stuff.*

"Behave now," she told the monkeys sternly, and turned to go.

But as she stepped back toward the gate, she realized that she'd forgotten to shut it.

And a very familiar gray tail was heading rapidly in the opposite direction.

"Spanky!" she gasped.

It's no use, Elizabeth thought two minutes later, careening around a corner in pursuit of the little gray monkey. She'd lost time when she'd locked the cage behind her. And she'd never suspected that monkeys could run so fast.

Elizabeth slowed down, rubbing her side. To her surprise, Spanky slowed down, too. "Chee, chee, chee!" he scolded her from about ten feet away. He raised his tail and waved it in the air. "Chee!"

Elizabeth took a deep breath. *Maybe if I walk slowly*, she thought. *Maybe I can fool him. I can certainly outsmart a monkey.* Pretending she was looking in the other direction, she took a few casual steps forward.

"Chee, chee, chee!" Spanky chattered.

Three more steps—two more—now! Elizabeth reached out, but her hands came up empty. Spanky had scurried away just in time. He sat cozily on a branch of an old pine tree, grinning down at her.

Elizabeth put her hands on her hips, exasperated. "Spanky!" she burst out.

But Spanky just chattered at her.

Elizabeth retraced her footsteps, looking for a sign of gray fluff. Spanky had completely disappeared, and she'd been searching for him for the last half hour. There was a hollow feeling at the pit of her stomach.

"Spanky?" she called, hoping against hope as she peered into a clump of bushes near the monkey house.

No answer.

He's got to be somewhere, Elizabeth thought, forcing herself to think reasonably. *He can't just have vanished into thin air!*

She took a deep breath. Standing back, she scanned the treetops. A few branches bobbed up and down in the light breeze, and the leaves rustled against each other. But there wasn't a monkey anywhere in sight.

"I'm really sorry, Madeleine," Elizabeth said, blinking back tears. It was nearly six o'clock, and no one had seen Spanky since his escape.

"Oh, he's probably playing one of his little games," Madeleine said consolingly. "We'll catch up with him, Elizabeth. Sooner or later."

"I hope so." Elizabeth shook her head. "I just feel awful about it. I'm so sorry, I really am."

"I know." Madeleine patted Elizabeth's shoulder. "Now go home and get some rest. We'll talk in the morning." She paused. "Isn't that your sister coming this way?"

Elizabeth looked eagerly down the path. "Jessica!" she called. Already she felt a little better. Elizabeth ran to her twin's side and buried her face in Jessica's shoulder. "I did the most horrible thing today," she said, her words muffled by Jessica's shirt. "I let Spanky escape."

"That's too bad," Jessica said absently. "Hey! Guess what Gus did today?"

Elizabeth straightened up. "Huh?"

"Gus," Jessica repeated. "You know, the little bear cub? Well, we were playing open-them-shut-them, and—"

The bear cub? Elizabeth frowned in confusion. "Jessica, I let a monkey escape from the zoo," she said urgently. "I'm really afraid they might fire me if he doesn't turn up."

"That's nice," Jessica said pleasantly. "Anyway, Justin says that bears don't really laugh, they just make noises that we think are like laughs, but I don't agree with him. When I was doing open-them-shut-them with Gus, he just laughed and laughed, and they sure sounded like real laughs to me."

Elizabeth stared at her twin in amazement. "Did you hear a single word I was saying?" she demanded.

Jessica started. "Huh?" she said. Elizabeth could see her sister's eyes slowly focus on her for a moment. Then they drifted off again. "So a little later, Gus was on the floor, and—"

Elizabeth dropped her sister's hand. "Oh, *you're* no help," she said bitterly and stormed off down the path.

"So he's just plain gone?" Melissa asked, her mouth a perfect circle of astonishment. She and Elizabeth were in the locker room on Friday morning.

"I guess so," Elizabeth said uncomfortably. She hadn't gotten much sleep last night. "Madeleine told me when I got here that no one had seen him all night."

"Bummer," Melissa commented. "You feel pretty down, huh?"

"That's the understatement of the century," Elizabeth agreed. Slowly she pulled her uniform out of her locker. "I should have locked the gate, but I didn't. I just plain blew it, that's all there is to it. I almost didn't bother to come in this morning."

"You don't suppose—" Melissa frowned.

"What?" Elizabeth asked glumly.

"Well, I'm thinking about what you said yesterday," Melissa went on. "You said monkeys aren't that smart. Remember?"

Elizabeth nodded as she took off her shoes. "So?"

"So it's just a guess, but do you think maybe Spanky is trying to pay you back for saying that?"

Elizabeth smiled despite herself. "You're not serious."

Melissa shrugged. "I know it seems weird. But some weird things are true. Couldn't it be that Spanky's trying to teach you a lesson by escaping?"

Elizabeth snorted. "Oh, *please*."

Eleven

"Gus, you're such a silly boy," Jessica said affectionately just before noon that Friday morning. She rubbed her nose against his. "And you're so smart, too."

Gus gurgled happily.

"Oh, you are so," Jessica went on, stroking his fur. "The way you sat up so straight when you saw me this morning. The way you're really learning to drink from the bottle. And—" She frowned. There was something else.

"Lunchtime, Jessica." Justin burst into the room.

"Lunch? Already?" Jessica couldn't believe how quickly time was passing. She started to her feet, but then sat down again, deciding she'd rather stay with Gus. "Oh—I'm not hungry," she said with a little wave of her hand. "I ate a big breakfast."

"Jessica," Justin said firmly, "you've been with Gus all morning. You need a break, and so does he. Go take, let's see, twenty minutes."

"Do I have to?" Jessica wiped a stray piece of hair out of her eyes and made a face.

"If you don't, I'll cancel your internship," Justin said, looking threateningly at Jessica.

He wouldn't really do that, would he? Jessica wondered. She kind of doubted it. Still, it was better to be safe than sorry. Reluctantly she dragged herself to her feet.

"Bye, Gus," she said, giving him a little kiss on the forehead. "I'll be back *real* soon."

As Jessica walked quickly toward the door, Gus began to whimper. Turning around, Jessica could see the cub stretching out his paws toward her, his eyes filling with tears.

Jessica blew him a kiss. *That's the other way I can tell he's so smart*, she thought. *He cries whenever I go anywhere without him!*

Elizabeth crumbled her napkin into a ball. She was sitting with Jessica at lunchtime in the zoo cafeteria. Usually Elizabeth loved the cafeteria, with its tables in the shape of tortoises and reindeer, but today she barely noticed her surroundings. She couldn't stop thinking about the missing monkey.

"You haven't seen Spanky this morning, have you?" Elizabeth ventured, peeling an orange.

"No," Jessica answered carelessly. "Hey, guess what Gus did this morning. It was so cute, you wouldn't even believe it."

"I'm sure it was really cute," Elizabeth mumbled. Normally Elizabeth would have been glad that Jessica was so excited about her internship. But right now she really needed to talk about Spanky. "It doesn't make sense. How could a monkey just vanish?"

"Hmm," Jessica said. "Speaking of vanishing, did I tell you about how I taught Gus to play peek-aboo this morning?"

Elizabeth shook her head, gazing wistfully across the cafeteria. "I really wish I could find him," she murmured.

"Find him?" Jessica gave Elizabeth a puzzled look. "Oh, he's easy to find. He's at the bear-habitat."

"He *is?*" Elizabeth's hopes leaped.

"Well, I *hope* he is." Jessica knit her brows. "Justin better not try to take that little bear away from me," she muttered half to herself, a dreamy look in her eyes.

Oh. Figures. Jessica was talking about Gus, not Spanky, Elizabeth realized. She sighed. "I guess if he doesn't turn up soon, I'll be spending my weekend looking all around town for him. It'll be a lot of bike riding," she said, making a face. "Or maybe I'll just take the bus."

Jessica snapped her head around and glared at Elizabeth. "You'll do *what?*" she snapped, starting to get up.

"Huh?" Elizabeth stared back at her sister. *What is she talking about?* "I said, I might be better off taking the bus to look for Spanky. What's with you?"

"Oh." Jessica settled herself back in her seat, a look of relief on her face. "I thought you said you would be taking *Gus.*"

*   *   *

"That's a barn owl," Bruce told Melissa after lunch. He kept a careful distance from the bird, but he let his hand brush casually against Melissa's as he pointed it out to her.

Melissa looked at him with what Bruce hoped was respect.

"See, you can tell barn owls from screech owls and hoot owls just by looking at their heads," Bruce went on. Last night, he'd studied some bird books, hoping to wow Melissa with his incredible knowledge. *As long as the owl stays on his perch, I'll be OK*, he thought. "Um—barn owls have really, really sharp beaks, see?"

"The other ones don't?" Melissa wanted to know.

The owl fluttered his wings ever so slightly. "Well, sure, but barn owls have really sharp claws, too," Bruce went on. He was having a hard time taking his eyes off the claws and the beak. "And did I mention their beaks, too?" Bruce asked. A chill ran up his spine. "They have to be incredibly sharp so they can tear apart the mice and other little animals they grab. With their really sharp claws, too, know what I mean?"

Melissa shivered. "Um, Bruce?"

"Yeah, the beaks just tear in and pull those animals apart," Bruce went on, unable to stop himself. In his mind's eye he could see the owl above him pulling open something else, too— *me*, he thought. "So they grab the mice with their razor-sharp claws, see, and—"

Melissa clapped her hands over her ears. "That's

totally gross, Bruce! Cut it out already!"

Bruce felt his face grow warm. "Oh, right. Guess that's enough bird facts for right now, huh?"

Melissa sighed, shaking her head.

"Hey, you two."

Bruce turned to see Pamela Moreland, the head bird keeper. Pamela studied Bruce and Melissa, her eyebrows raised. "Hope I'm not interrupting anything," she said slyly.

Bruce turned beet red. "You aren't," he said quickly.

"Good, because I have a job for one of you." Pamela consulted her clipboard. "A shipment of eggs has just come in. They'll be due to hatch sometime early next week, and I wondered if one of you would be interested in watching them. You know, measuring them, turning them, just making sure nothing happens."

Bruce considered. Watching eggs sounded pretty boring, but eggs didn't have monstrous wings and enormous razor-sharp claws. He smiled. *Yup, it'll be a no-brainer.*

Bruce was about to volunteer when Melissa spoke up.

"Bruce will," she said.

"I—how did you know?" Bruce turned to her in surprise.

Melissa smiled. "Oh, just a lucky guess."

Bruce frowned. *It's like she knows that I'm—concerned—about birds or something. How'd she figure that out?*

*   *   *

As she rode her bike home that afternoon, Elizabeth couldn't get her mind off Spanky. No one had seen him. Not even a glimpse. She couldn't believe she'd let this happen. Why hadn't she been more alert?

She turned onto Calico Drive, the street where the Wakefields lived. Suddenly she had a horrible thought. *What if he's dead?* She couldn't imagine what she'd do if—

Abruptly Elizabeth jammed on the brakes. *What was that?* She skidded to a stop just behind a parked car, but she barely noticed. Craning her neck, she peered up at the sign that said CALICO DRIVE.

Hanging from the sign was a very familiar little gray monkey!

"Spanky!" Elizabeth shouted. Relief flooded her heart. "Come down from there this minute!"

Spanky swung back and forth and chattered happily at her. Elizabeth peered at the Calico Drive sign—which, at the moment, didn't actually read Calico Drive. Spanky's paws were covering some of the letters, so that instead of Calico Drive, the sign spelled out ali ve.

Coincidence, Elizabeth thought, then stamped her foot. "Spanky!"

"Chee, chee, chee," the little monkey scolded her.

The street sign was far too high for Elizabeth to reach. *I could wait all day for him to come down,* she thought. *Or maybe I should—*

"Wait right there!" she called to the monkey,

pedaling as hard as she could for home. Bursting into the house, she picked up the telephone and dialed the zoo.

Now we've got you for sure, you little sneak! she thought affectionately.

"You're sure you saw him?" Madeleine frowned up at the street sign on the corner.

Elizabeth nibbled anxiously on her fingernail. "I—I know I did. I really did." Half an hour had gone by since Elizabeth had called the zoo. But Spanky had disappeared once again. "He was standing right there." She gestured with her finger to the exact spot. "I saw him, but when I went to call, he must have climbed up a tree or something."

Madeleine nodded, then checked her watch. "I have to be getting back to the zoo. Tell you what. If you see him again—and you might—don't let him out of your sight. Send someone else to call if you have to, but watch him constantly. OK?"

"OK," Elizabeth mumbled.

"Atta girl." Madeleine squeezed Elizabeth's shoulder and got into her car. Sadly, Elizabeth watched her drive off.

So close, she told herself miserably. *And now he's gone again.*

"It was so weird," Elizabeth said later on that afternoon. She was sitting in Casey's ice cream parlor with her friends Amy Sutton and Maria Slater, enjoying a thick milk shake. "One moment Spanky was there, and the next—" She snapped her fingers. "Poof!"

"He was history, huh?" Maria's eyes twinkled as she licked her ice cream cone.

"Totally gone," Elizabeth said. "I guess I'll have to figure out a way *not* to mention Spanky when I give my presentation next Thursday."

"Next Thursday?" Amy looked blank.

"You remember," Maria reminded her. "A few of the interns will talk about what they did, and then we get the good stuff—a pizza party." She took another lick.

"Oh, right." Amy twirled a lock of hair. "What color is Spanky, anyway?"

Elizabeth was about to answer, when suddenly there was a commotion in the back room.

"Get out of here, whatever you are!" Mr. Casey shouted. There was a clang as a pot came flying forward and bounced against the base of the counter. Then there was a very familiar "Chee, chee, chee!"

"Spanky!" Elizabeth burst out. She'd know that sound anywhere. A second later the grinning face of the little gray monkey appeared above the counter. *Almost as though he was waiting to be announced before making his appearance*, Elizabeth thought with a giggle. *Like a game show host or something!*

Amy rose from her stool to get a better look. "He's so adorable!"

Adorable? Elizabeth thought, rolling her eyes. *Yeah, right!*

"Chee, chee, chee!" Spanky chattered, waving a finger.

Don't leave him, Elizabeth ordered herself, remembering Madeleine's words. "Block him off if he tries to escape," she commanded, dashing for the phone.

Spanky hopped along the counter, grabbing handfuls of cherries and chocolate chips and stuffing them into his mouth. Elizabeth dialed the fire department as quickly as she could. *They'd get here before Madeleine*, she told herself as she explained the problem into the phone.

Hanging up, she saw that the monkey had clambered to the ceiling and was swinging joyfully from the light fixture. "Spanky!" she ordered. "You come down right now!"

Showing his teeth, Spanky threw a cherry at Elizabeth's nose.

"Hey!" she cried in indignation.

"You know this monkey?" Mr. Casey came out into the front room and gazed, astonished, at the creature on the ceiling.

Spanky took careful aim and tossed a chocolate chip right into Mr. Casey's open mouth. "Chee, chee!" he chattered in celebration, twisting his body back and forth in the air.

Mr. Casey gaped. "What in the world—" He broke off as sirens sounded in the distance.

Elizabeth glanced anxiously out the window. *Hurry*, she thought.

The little monkey cocked his head. Then, with one smooth motion, he vaulted over the counter and headed for the open door. "Catch him!" Elizabeth shouted frantically. Maria, who was standing nearby, dived and came up with—air.

"Oh, no!" Elizabeth squeezed her eyes shut. She couldn't believe how close they'd come.

But when the firefighters arrived thirty seconds later, Spanky was gone. Again.

"So what country are you living in these days, sis?" Steven looked at Jessica across the kitchen counter. He and the twins were cleaning up Friday night after dinner.

"Hmm?" Jessica responded, gazing into space.

Elizabeth yanked open the dishwasher and sighed. She couldn't believe how spacey Jessica was acting lately.

"How come you never laugh at my jokes anymore?" Steven went on. "What's so exciting at the zoo that you won't even listen to me, huh?"

"She's fallen in love with a baby bear," Elizabeth explained in a grumpy voice.

"Oh!" Steven leaned closer to Jessica. "I get it! You've given up on boys altogether, huh? You're going for a bear instead?" He growled. "Well, maybe that's not such a bad idea. What's the lucky bear's name?"

Jessica raised a dreamy eye toward her brother. "Gus."

"Gus, huh?" Steven snorted. "I can see it now— 'I'd like you to meet my new brother-in-law, Gus.'" He pretended to shake hands. "Gee, pleased to meet you, Gus. Looking good, buddy. You must be having a good fur day." He laughed uproariously. "Like a bad-hair day—get it?"

Elizabeth rolled her eyes. "Jess, hand me that plate over there, please."

"You don't understand, Steven," Jessica said pleasantly, not making a move for the plate. "This little cub needs me, that's all. He doesn't have a mother anymore. I'm going in over the weekend to spend time with him."

Steven hit his forehead. "I didn't realize my sister was capable of such compassion. Since when did you ever care about poor abandoned animals?"

Jessica shrugged. "Since now," she said calmly.

Elizabeth reached across the counter herself and rinsed off the plate. She had to agree that Jessica was acting pretty out-of-the-ordinary. *I'm supposed to be the one who's all excited about animals*, she thought, an empty feeling at the pit of her stomach. *Jessica was the one who didn't want to do the internship at all. And now she's got a baby bear to cuddle. And all I've got is a stupid monkey to chase around town.*

She jammed the plates into the dishwasher. *Not that I'm jealous or anything,* she told herself quickly.

She glanced at her sister, who was humming happily to herself.

Well, not a lot anyway.

Twelve

The eggs are sure better than the birds, Bruce thought happily on Monday afternoon. To his surprise, he found he was really enjoying studying them. They were all different sizes and colors, but they were all pretty much the same shape. *Kind of round at one end and kind of oval at the other,* he thought, examining one of the biggest ones closely.

Wait a minute.

Bruce leaned closer. There was a small crack in the side of the egg. "Bummer," he said aloud, touching the egg gently to see if it felt weak. It did.

"Too bad," Bruce sighed, wrinkling his forehead. "Guess I should probably throw it out or something."

"Throw what out?"

Melissa came up from behind. She rested her arm gently on the back of Bruce's chair.

"This egg," he said, pointing. "See the crack? I think it's bogus."

"Bogus?" Melissa looked from the egg to Bruce and back. "What are you talking about?"

Bruce frowned. "Well, it's, like, breaking into pieces," he explained with exaggerated politeness. "See, there's a crack *here*, and it feels really thin *here*, and—"

A small smile played on the corners of Melissa's mouth. "Actually, the egg isn't falling apart. It's about to hatch!"

About to hatch? Bruce peered at the egg once more. "Oh, yeah," he grunted, not quite daring to look Melissa in the eye. "Knew it all the time."

Melissa bent down and studied the egg a little more closely. "This is so neat. We're going to get to see a baby bird pretty soon!"

"Great," Bruce said as enthusiastically as he could manage. He stared at the crack and willed it not to get any larger.

Volunteer for something innocent like egg duty, he thought, a shiver of dread creeping slowly up his back, *and what happens?*

He bit his lip, hard.

The stupid egg turns into a—

Bird.

You guys still don't look too smart, Elizabeth thought as she fed the big brown monkeys. *Of course, Spanky did seem to know what the sirens meant yesterday. And it was pretty weird the way he just turned up on my street.*

"Chee, chee, chee!" a big monkey scolded Elizabeth. With a start she realized she'd forgotten to put out the carrots. "You must be—" She frowned, trying to remember the name of the monkey who especially liked carrots. "Miss Milwaukee?"

The monkey frowned back.

"Oh, Howler, that's right!" Elizabeth exclaimed. But the monkey just put its hands on its hips and stared.

Let's see—Jafiri—Bullwinkle—Henry the Second— "Kiyesha!" she exclaimed triumphantly. The monkey in front of her jumped up and down, excitement all over her face. "Here you go, sweetie." Elizabeth dropped a bunch of carrots onto the floor.

Elizabeth couldn't help smiling as she moved along. *But lots of animals know their names—that's not any big deal. And just because Spanky showed up a couple of times, that doesn't prove that monkeys are smart,* she mused. *I mean, of course he'd prefer freedom to the zoo. And of course he'd run away when he saw me, or when he heard strange noises.*

She left the cage and locked the door behind her.

Next time, she decided, she wouldn't make any phone calls. She'd try to catch him herself.

"If there is a next time," she said aloud, her voice sounding thin among the chatter of dozens of monkeys.

"Which I seriously doubt!"

"Un-be-lievable!"

Steven stopped outside Gus's cage and stared at his sister rocking the little bear in the corner. He'd dropped by on his way to the beach, hoping to see this for himself.

"Nice fashion statement, Jessica!" he called, grabbing the bars and looking in.

Jessica looked up from playing patty-cake with Gus. "Oh, hi, Steven," she called. "Good to see you."

Steven frowned. *Good to see you?* This wasn't any fun. Jessica was supposed to be the twin who was easy to tease. He decided to try again. "That green uniform sure matches your eyes!"

Jessica turned her attention back to Gus. "Who's Jessie's little boy?" she gurgled.

Steven stared in fascination. He'd never seen Jessica like this before. "Gee!" he shouted, rattling the bars of the cage. "It sure smells like a zoo in here! Ha, ha, ha!" *There. That ought to get her.*

"Ignore that loser, boy," Jessica said primly. Gus snuggled up against her ear.

Steven bit his lip and thought hard. "Can I hold Junior next?" he squeaked, holding out his hands. "Isn't he just adorable?"

"Oh, you funny little boy," Jessica clucked, grabbing Gus in a tight hug. The little bear moaned happily, and Jessica laughed.

Steven heaved an enormous sigh. Jessica was having way too much fun for his taste. "What's so funny anyway?" he asked.

Jessica looked up at him, her eyes dancing. "Gus just wet—right onto the leg of my uniform!" she said happily.

"He what?" Steven stared at his sister in astonishment.

Jessica beamed. "I said that Gus—"

But Steven didn't wait around to hear it again.

No doubt about it—aliens had taken over his sister's body. Shaking his head, he bolted for the zoo entrance.

That egg really is about to hatch, Bruce said to himself a little later on. This was *not* good news, not at all. Judging from the size of the egg, the bird would be pretty big. *Do newborn baby birds have big claws?* he wondered.

"Hey, Melissa?" he asked.

"Yeah?" Melissa looked up from feeding a starling.

"What kind of a bird do you think will come out of this?" Bruce asked, trying to sound casual.

Melissa glanced at the egg. "Probably something big," she said thoughtfully.

Bruce stifled a shudder. "But what?"

"I don't know," Melissa admitted. "I think I'd guess a raptor."

"A raptor?" Bruce's eyes opened very wide. A picture of *Tyrannosaurus rex* flashed into his mind. *T. rex* with open bloody jaws. He took a step back. "You mean it's a dinosaur?"

"A dinosaur?" Melissa fixed Bruce with a look.

Bruce nodded, going pale. In his mind the *T. rex* lumbered slowly forward. "You know, like the basketball team. The Toronto Raptors. Right?"

Melissa's lips twitched. "Why do you think a dinosaur might come out of that egg?" she asked gently. "There haven't been any dinosaurs for thousands of years."

"Oh." Bruce realized his imagination had run

away with him. He took a deep breath. "I knew that," he said quickly. "But you said—"

"Raptor just means predator, Bruce," Melissa explained. "An animal that catches prey, like a hawk or an eagle. You don't really think that a dinosaur could hatch out of that egg, do you?"

Bruce stared at the egg again. "Of course not," he muttered after a moment. Clearing his throat, he casually brushed his hair out of his face. "I just wondered if maybe you thought so."

An hour later Bruce watched as a razor-sharp beak poked through the eggshell and began to make little sawing motions. Melissa was off somewhere else in the aviary, and Bruce was all alone. His heart was pounding. *It's hatching,* he thought, wondering if he should try to protect himself or something.

Then he squared his shoulders. *Be real, Patman,* he told himself. *No reason to be afraid of a little tiny bird!*

The crack was growing larger, and the beak seemed to be moving faster. A moment later the egg broke neatly into pieces. Bruce drew in his breath. There, on the inside, was the tiniest, fuzziest, wettest creature he had ever seen in his life. Its head was scrunched down, completely buried in its feathers.

Totally goofy, Bruce thought, watching the shivering ball of fuzz. He suspected Melissa and those Wakefield twins would think it was cute. But as for him, he thought it looked better as an egg.

In fact, the more Bruce stared at it, the more he disliked it. *It's stupid looking,* he thought with a sneer. *And it's a bird. And just as soon as it's old enough to move, it will probably try to bite me.* He stared at the huddled little chick with distrust.

The chick moved.

Out of the downy fluff, a little head appeared. The baby bird blinked its eyes open. Once—twice—three times. It stared directly at Bruce and made a tiny sound.

"Don't come near me," Bruce told it sourly.

The baby chick hopped slowly forward, directly toward Bruce. It squeaked hopefully. After a few hops, it fell down, then picked itself up and continued to hop forward.

Uh-oh, Bruce told himself. Quickly he walked around to the other side of the incubator.

The bird tilted its head and made a mournful squeak. Then it fell down once again. This time, when it got back to its feet, it was facing the other way. "Eeep!" the bird chirped joyfully, and began to hop toward Bruce once again.

It likes me, Bruce thought in disgust as the bird slowly made its way toward him. *The look on its face—the way it hops—*

Great.

Bruce slumped forward and shook his head. "There ain't no justice," he mumbled. For a solid week he'd been trying to get the attention of a really hot chick—Melissa. And now it seemed that a different kind of chick had the hots for him.

"Eeep?" A wing brushed Bruce's nose.

With a scream, he bounded back. "Well, you can forget about it," he told the chick, pointing an accusing forefinger in its direction. "Because I'm just plain not interested! Not interested, do you understand?"

Funny. He could have sworn the baby bird looked downright—disappointed.

Thirteen

On Tuesday, Bruce took his time getting to the zoo. He took his time getting into his uniform. And he took his time walking to the aviary. He didn't want to admit it, even to himself, but he was trying hard to avoid that little baby bird.

Maybe it will have forgotten me completely, he thought as he walked through the aviary gate.

But probably not.

As Bruce walked over to the eggs, he felt like a prisoner condemned to death. He looked down into the incubator. *Good*, he thought when he saw the chick huddled in a corner. *It's asleep. Now I can—*

"Eeep!" the bird squeaked, standing up quickly and fluffing up its wings. Bruce drew back a little. *Just in case*, he told himself. "Eeep!" The chick headed straight for him, its legs much steadier than yesterday.

Just great, Bruce thought bitterly, wondering

what in the world he had ever done to deserve this.

"Eeep, eeep, eeep!" the chick chirped. To Bruce's dismay, it hopped onto his arm and climbed quickly up to his shoulder. "Get off!" he commanded, gingerly reaching out and giving it a little whack with his finger.

The bird was amazingly light. It tumbled to the bottom of the incubator. "Eeep, eeep!" it squeaked again, and hopped onto his hand once more.

Funny-looking thing, Bruce thought angrily, swatting at it even harder. *Why don't you just go away, huh?*

Melissa appeared at his side. "Oh, it's so adorable!" she squealed, eyeing the chick as it struggled to its feet.

She sounds just like the chick, Bruce thought grumpily.

The chick dipped and swayed and hopped right onto his hand again.

"That's so sweet," Melissa said with a laugh. "Bruce, you're so lucky!"

Bruce could hear the envy in her tone. "Yeah? Well, you can have it!" he exclaimed. The chick had reached his shoulder, so he pushed it off once more.

"Bruce Patman!" Melissa put her hands on her hips and stared. "I can't believe you just did that! Why don't you try being nice for once in your life?"

"Eeep, eeep," the chick scolded, looking at Bruce reproachfully from the incubator.

Bruce's face burned, but he wasn't about to show Melissa how embarrassed he was. "Because," he grunted. The bird hopped onto his sleeve. This time it dug its claws into the fabric and held on tight. "Come on, bird," he said in what he hoped was a kind and gentle voice. "Let go—come on—"

One thing's for sure, he told himself, wincing. *A one-day-old bird can grab like crazy!*

Melissa began to laugh.

"What's so funny?" Bruce demanded, trying to free his sleeve.

"Remember science class last year?" Melissa grinned. "When we studied birds? This chick's imprinted on you!"

"Imprinted?" Bruce shook his sleeve, trying to shake off the chick. "What do you mean?"

"It thinks you're its mother!" Melissa dissolved into giggles.

Bruce felt his blood boil. "That's ridiculous," he snapped, finally yanking the claws off his sleeve. He dropped the bird on the table. With a squeak, the bird ran back for the shelter of Bruce's arm.

Melissa giggled behind her hand. "See what I mean? It needs you."

As he eyed the bird, Bruce felt a wave of dread washing over him. He hated to admit it, but it looked like Melissa was right. *It thinks I'm its mother,* Bruce repeated silently. *Its mother!*

Good grief!

"Monkeys often amaze scientists with their clever behavior," Elizabeth read with a sigh.

Well, if they're so clever, she thought, shutting her book with a thump, *how come I haven't noticed?*

Elizabeth was sitting in the public library that

afternoon. She'd taken some time to do some research for her presentation on Thursday. Most of what she was finding out was interesting. But it did seem as if everyone who'd ever studied monkeys thought they were brilliant.

Except herself.

More and more the monkeys reminded her of her classmates. The loud, obnoxious ones made her think of some of the boys she knew. The leaders never groomed anyone else and were mean to the ones they didn't like—*just like a few of the Unicorns*, Elizabeth told herself.

Every time Madeleine pointed out something a monkey was doing and called it intelligent, Elizabeth could always see a different explanation: instinct, or meanness, or just plain showing off. "It's not like they communicate with each other," she murmured aloud, stretching. "Or work together, or solve problems, or—"

Out of the corner of her eye, Elizabeth saw a flash of gray.

Huh? Dropping the book, she squinted across the reading room. There, curled up on one of the bookshelves, sat—

"Spanky!"

The little monkey grinned when he heard his name. "Chee, chee," he said very softly, then put his finger to his lips just like a librarian shushing a customer.

Elizabeth looked around. The room was empty. *I'll have to handle this one myself,* she thought. "Hi, Spanky," she said quietly, walking forward.

The little monkey yawned.

This should be easy, Elizabeth thought. She took a

step nearer. "I'll give you carrots," she promised, pretending to munch on a long skinny carrot.

Spanky yawned again.

Elizabeth could practically touch Spanky now. She leaned against a table and stretched out her arms. "Come on, boy."

Spanky closed his eyes and gave a little snore.

Easy as pie, Elizabeth thought. All her troubles would be over soon. Climbing onto the table without making a noise, she reached out—

And grabbed an empty bookshelf.

"Spanky!" Elizabeth whirled around, just in time to see Spanky's tail disappearing through the open door. By the time Elizabeth managed to untangle herself from the bookshelf, Spanky had vanished completely.

"Forty-one, forty-two, forty-three," Bruce counted. Gently he touched each egg still in the incubator, trying hard to ignore the little bird hopping around on his shoulder. He'd knocked it away about a dozen times, but no matter what, the bird always hopped back up.

"Hey, Mom!" Melissa said teasingly.

"Don't call me that," Bruce mumbled. "Besides, you made me lose count," he added accusingly.

Melissa's eyes danced. "You know, if you're going to be that chick's mother, you really ought to give it a name. It's the least you can do."

Bruce knew she was only joking, but he just wasn't in the mood for games. "All right," he agreed. He gave the chick a little swat and tried to think up the worst name he could. *Loser—Pestface—Nerdy? Nope.* "Drumstick," he said aloud. "I'll call it Drumstick."

Melissa frowned. "You mean like the thing you hit a drum with?"

Bruce shook his head. "No. Drumstick, like in 'finger-lickin' good'?" *Chomp, chomp,* he thought, glaring at the little bird.

A shadow crossed Melissa's face. "That's disgusting," she said after a moment. Shaking her head, she walked away.

Bruce bit his lip as he watched her go. There was an uneasy feeling in the pit of his stomach, a feeling he wasn't used to and didn't quite know what to do about. Just for a moment he thought about calling her back and—

"Eeep?" Drumstick asked.

Bruce sighed in exasperation. "Stupid bird," he muttered. It was all the dumb bird's fault. Of course it was. If it hadn't been for the bird, Melissa wouldn't have tried to tease him. If there hadn't been any bird, he'd never have named it Drumstick. And anyway, Melissa didn't have to be so snotty about the name. It was a perfectly good name. Sure it was. *Yeah, it's all the bird's fault,* he thought.

He took a deep breath. Somehow he didn't feel a lot better.

"Well, it's not my fault, anyway!" he said to Drumstick, giving the chick an especially hard glare.

Fourteen

◇

"You're getting so big," Jessica whispered happily to Gus on Wednesday morning. She hefted the baby bear into a sitting position. "But not too big to rock and cuddle!"

Gus rubbed his cheek against the shoulder of Jessica's uniform.

"And you're eating solid food," Jessica went on, her eyes sparkling. "And you can stand on two legs now, too!" Grasping Gus's front paws, she raised him so he stood only on his back legs. "See?"

Gus gurgled, and the corners of his lips seemed to curve up into a smile.

"Come on." Jessica carefully set the cub's front legs back onto the ground. "Let's play some ball." She pulled an old tennis ball out of her uniform pocket while Gus scuttled to the side of the cage.

"Ready?" Jessica gently rolled the ball toward Gus.

"Grr!" Gus growled at the ball, the hair on his

back rising as it came closer. Then he stopped the ball with his paw and tried to bite it.

"No, silly," Jessica told him. "You hit it. With your paw. Like this." She demonstrated with her own hand.

Gus growled again and hit the ball with his nose. It rolled a few feet and came to a stop.

"Well, sort of!" Jessica told him. She stood up and headed for the ball.

Justin's voice floated in from the outside of the cage, where he was standing with a forest service ranger. *The same one who helped bring Gus in*, Jessica thought dimly. She could make out just a few words of their conversation.

"Blah blah blah blah temporary," she heard Justin saying.

"Blah blah blah blah Saturday," the ranger agreed. Or maybe it was "batter play."

Jessica rolled the ball to Gus again. "Some people talk about the most boring things, don't they Gus?"

"Grr!" Gus said again. This time he waited till the ball was almost on top of him. Then his eyes grew wide with fear, and he ran into Jessica's arms.

Jessica laughed. "You are a silly." She held him close against her chest. "You know what, Gus?" she asked. "When I grow up and have a baby of my own, I want him to be exactly like you!"

Monkeys sure make a lot of mess, Elizabeth thought, training the hose on an especially filthy part of the monkey cage. She'd been hosing the cage for half an hour already, and it looked like the job might take the whole morning.

Elizabeth moved the stream of water a little to the left—but suddenly all she had was a trickle.

"Huh?" she asked aloud. She shook the hose up and down just in case something had gotten stuck inside. Nothing fell out. *Guess I'll look inside*, she thought. She turned the nozzle toward her face— and a jet of water spurted out.

"Hey!" she sputtered, dropping the hose and frantically wiping water from her face.

"Chee, chee, chee!"

Elizabeth forced her eyes open. She was wet all over. Turning around, she saw three big monkeys chattering at her. One of them held a section of the hose in its hand. As she watched, the monkey deftly kinked the hose. The water at her feet instantly slowed to a trickle again.

"You did that!" Elizabeth said in amazement.

"Chee, chee, chee!" As Elizabeth took a step forward, the monkey dropped the hose. All three of them ran to sit on the window, too high up for Elizabeth to reach.

"Well, of all the nerve!" Elizabeth wiped soaked strands of hair out of her eyes. Her shoes were sodden. Shading her eyes, she glared at the monkeys in the window. "That wasn't very nice," she said, hands on her hips.

"Chee, chee, chee!" The monkeys looked out the window and started to chatter again. Then they looked down again as if expecting her to come join them.

Elizabeth suspected they were setting another

trap, but she couldn't help wondering exactly what they wanted. She walked slowly over. "What is it?" she asked cautiously.

"Chee, chee, chee!" The largest monkey pointed.

Elizabeth gasped. On the other side of the window was Spanky! The little gray monkey grinned and raised one paw.

Elizabeth's mind raced. *He's not going to escape this time!* she thought. "Madeleine!" she shouted. But as she started for the cage entrance, the three big monkeys scurried across her path. Before she realized what was happening, Elizabeth fell heavily to the floor.

"Chee, chee, chee!" Monkeys from around the cage came bounding over. They leaped happily all around her.

"Ow!" Elizabeth cried, struggling to her feet. She pushed away Miss Milwaukee and tried to unhook Jafiri's legs from around her neck. "Stop it, you guys!"

"What's the problem?" Madeleine's voice rang out through the loud chattering of monkeys.

Elizabeth took a gulp of air, trying to collect herself. Capuchin, or maybe Henry the Second, pulled a handful of her hair. "Spanky's outside the window!" she gasped.

Madeleine dashed toward the door as Elizabeth tried to free her hair. "Let go!" she demanded.

All at once one of the monkeys gave a little whistle. To her surprise, Elizabeth found that she was suddenly free again.

"Well, that wasn't much fun," she told the monkeys, standing up and dusting herself off. "I sure hope Madeleine caught Spanky!" Lurching to the cage entrance, she opened the door and locked it securely behind her.

Madeleine was walking toward her. "Did you catch him?" Elizabeth asked hopefully.

Madeleine shook her head. "He's nowhere in sight."

Elizabeth sighed with frustration. "I can't believe it. It's been, like, four times now."

"Elizabeth." Madeleine put her hand on Elizabeth's shoulder. "Maybe you just thought you saw Spanky," she said kindly. "You've been wanting to find him so badly, after all."

"But I *do* keep seeing him," Elizabeth insisted. She looked at Madeleine pleadingly. "I really do!"

Madeleine patted her back. "All right," she said. But she didn't meet Elizabeth's gaze.

"Hey, cut that out!" Bruce snapped later on that afternoon. He was turning three of the largest eggs so they would be warm on all sides when Drumstick began nuzzling his forearm. "Can't you see I'm busy?"

"She's only little, Bruce," Melissa said quietly. "You don't have to be so mean to her."

Bruce glanced from Melissa to the little ball of fluff and back. "How do you know it's a girl?" he asked.

Melissa shrugged. "Girls can always tell when animals are girls."

Oh. Bruce stared again at Drumstick.

"I mean, look at her," Melissa went on. "So soft and innocent and all."

She does look innocent, Bruce thought, shaking his head. *At first glance, anyway. All fuzzy and soft and frail.*

But Bruce couldn't forget that deep down, Drumstick was a bird. *One of these days,* he thought, *she will grow up to be a humongous creature with a razor-sharp beak and huge claws.*

"Elizabeth?" Mrs. Wakefield called as soon as Elizabeth let herself in the house that afternoon. "Is that you? You're home early today."

"I know." Elizabeth had left the zoo about half an hour earlier than usual. "There's a project I need to work on." She walked into the living room and came to a halt. In front of her sat an impossibly thin man wearing the skinniest necktie Elizabeth had ever seen. Next to him was a woman whose hair was piled on her head in elaborate spirals. *I've seen pictures of women with hair like that,* she recalled. *But they all lived about a hundred and fifty years ago!*

"These are my clients, Mr. and Mrs. Tweed," Mrs. Wakefield said. "My daughter Elizabeth."

"Pleased to meet you," Elizabeth said, smiling tightly.

Mrs. Tweed stuck her nose in the air. "Likewise, I'm sure."

"We were just going out," Mrs. Wakefield told her, "so you'll have the house to yourself until Steven gets home. Have fun with your project. Is it interesting?"

"I guess you could say that," Elizabeth told her. "Just hoping to outsmart a certain monkey I know!"

"A monkey?" Mr. Tweed peered over the top of his rimless glasses. He looked in confusion from Elizabeth to Mrs. Wakefield and back again.

"Disgusting little things," Mrs. Tweed sniffed. "Mrs. Wakefield, surely you don't allow monkeys in your home?"

Mrs. Wakefield frowned. "No, of course not," she said with a little laugh. "Um—I suspect she's talking about her brother." She stood up and waited for the Tweeds to do the same. "You know how brothers and sisters are."

"Indeed not," Mrs. Tweed huffed, struggling to her feet. Every single strand of hair remained firmly in place. "I am proud to say that Oswald and I were both only children."

"As is our daughter, little Felicia," Mr. Tweed put in. His necktie looked even skinnier now that he was standing up.

"I see." Mrs. Wakefield took a deep breath and plastered a smile on her face. "Well, my children often refer to each other as monkeys and things like that—all in fun, of course," she added quickly as she led the way out of the room.

"Good heavens." Mrs. Tweed gave a delicate shudder. "I can't imagine why little Felicia always wanted to be part of a large family," she added as she disappeared through the door, her husband trailing along behind.

Clomp, clomp, clomp. Steven strode heavily into the kitchen an hour later. "Hey, Elizabeth!" he greeted his sister. "How do you like my new work boots, huh? Bought 'em this morning."

"That's nice." Elizabeth didn't turn around but continued staring out the window. She'd set a trap for Spanky, and now all she had to do was wait.

Steven opened the refrigerator door. "A real bargain," he crowed. "And they almost even fit."

"Uh-huh." Was that a gray tail twitching out at the corner of the yard? Elizabeth stiffened—and relaxed. *Just a branch.*

"What'd you do with all the bananas?" Steven demanded.

"The bananas?" Elizabeth glanced at her brother guiltily. "Oh—they're outside."

"Outside?" A frown creased Steven's face. "What are they doing there?"

Elizabeth blushed slightly. "Um, well, actually, I'm trying to catch a monkey."

"A monkey?" Steven eyed her skeptically.

Elizabeth smiled. She had to admit, she enjoyed baffling Steven. "This monkey at the zoo escaped"— Elizabeth saw no reason to mention exactly *how* he'd escaped—"and I'm trying to catch him."

"Escaped?" Steven raised an eyebrow. "So that's why you're so bummed out about your internship?"

"Well—yeah." Elizabeth was a little surprised that her brother had figured out her mood.

"I knew there was something," Steven observed, tapping his forehead meaningfully. "Jessica's the one who hates animals, and you're the one who's moping around all the time." He narrowed his eyes. "Bet you didn't think I'd notice."

Elizabeth shrugged. "Well, actually—"

"That's what I thought," Steven said huffily. "So you're trying to catch this monkey with bananas?"

"That's right." Elizabeth watched as Steven reached into the freezer and took out a carton of ice cream. "See, he keeps showing himself and then running off and hiding, so I figured I'd set up a trap in the yard."

"Cool," Steven commented. "What'd you do—dig a pit so he'd fall in?"

Elizabeth shook her head. "I used a big crate and I tipped it up so it was balanced on a little stick," she explained, sketching the box in the air. "Then underneath, way at the back, I put a bunch of food. Bananas and Twinkies and a peanut butter sandwich—things like that."

"Twinkies?" Steven scratched his head. "Monkeys like Twinkies?"

Elizabeth suppressed a grin. "Monkeys *love* Twinkies. I read it in a book yesterday."

Steven looked thoughtful as he reached into the cupboard for a bowl. "So if he goes for the food—"

"Then he knocks over the stick and the box traps him," Elizabeth filled in. "I checked it. He's not smart enough to figure out a way around the stick."

"Let me see." Steven walked across to the window and thrust back the curtains. "Pretty cool," he said after a moment. "By the way, what's that monkey look like?"

"Gray," Elizabeth replied. "Kind of small, a long tail—"

"You mean like that one?" Steven stepped back and jerked his thumb toward the yard. Her heart racing, Elizabeth darted forward and looked out.

"Oh, no!" she screamed in frustration.

The box was still tilted up on the stick.

And Spanky was dashing mischievously across the lawn, his front paws full of Twinkies.

"No wonder you couldn't catch him," Steven scoffed a few minutes later. He and Elizabeth had come out into the yard, but Spanky was gone. Gingerly he touched the crate. "It's too stable, see. It won't fall."

"It—won't?" Elizabeth looked at the crate helplessly.

"Nope," Steven told her authoritatively. "A monkey could easily get through this."

"Oh," Elizabeth said in a small voice.

Steven inspected the stick. "Hey, look. He left the bananas."

Elizabeth frowned slightly. "That's weird. You'd think if he were scrounging for food, he'd take everything."

"He probably wanted to save some for me," Steven said, flexing his fingers. "That's what I like—a monkey with manners." He carefully snuck his hand in the trap from one side and groped for the bananas. "Got 'em!" he crowed.

Just at that moment, his sleeve brushed the stick. Elizabeth gasped as the heavy wooden crate fell firmly against Steven's arm.

Fifteen

◇

"Oh, Gus!" Jessica called as she pushed open the door to Gus's cage on Thursday morning. "Gus!"

The little cub was nowhere in sight. Jessica frowned. Gus had always come to the gate the moment he spotted her through the bars.

"Gus!" Jessica put her hands on her hips. *I bet he's trying to play a joke on me,* she thought with a wry smile. *Probably I shouldn't have taught him to play hide-and-seek yesterday!* "All right, where are you?" she demanded, tapping her foot with mock impatience.

The cage was still as could be.

Jessica bit her lip. Gus hadn't been very good at hide-and-seek, she reminded herself. There weren't many places to hide to begin with, and Gus seemed unable to stay in one place for long. *He must be behind that tree stump,* she thought at last, remembering Gus's favorite hiding place during the game. She walked over and peered down behind the stump. "Gus!"

There was a tennis ball, a piece of string, and some leftover vegetables.

But no baby bear.

Where is he? Jessica thought, desperately scanning the parking lot for Justin's Jeep. Both Gus and Justin had been gone since she arrived at the zoo three hours ago, and no one seemed to know exactly where.

Jessica shaded her eyes against the glare of the sun, willing the next car to be Justin's.

Yes! The car pulled to a stop. Jessica recognized the bumper stickers right away: Support The Right To Arm Bears, Hug A Bear, and Bear-ly Making It. But she had eyes for only one thing.

"Gus!" she burst out, dashing forward almost before Justin had turned the engine off. She thrust open the door and scooped up the cub from the passenger seat with one quick motion. "Where have you been?" she asked Justin accusingly.

Gus sighed happily and nestled into Jessica's arms.

"At the vet's." Justin didn't smile. "We had to wait for quite a while."

"Oh." Jessica's eyes widened. "Is he—is he all right?"

"Just fine," Justin reported. "So he'll be all ready for his relocation this weekend."

"His—" Jessica stared up at Justin. Her blood suddenly ran cold. "His what?"

"His relocation." Justin shrugged. "You know.

When we take him back to the wild. On Saturday."

Jessica stared in horror at Justin. "Back to the wild? What in the world are you talking about?" she almost shouted, wrapping her arms protectively around Gus.

"I'm really sorry, Jessica," Justin said in the bear-habitat office a few minutes later. "I thought I explained it to you earlier. But maybe that was before you met Gus." He made a helpless gesture with his hands. "I guess you weren't interested then."

Jessica wiped tears from her eyes. Gus slept on her lap, his chest peacefully rising and falling. "But, Justin—"

"I'm sorry." Justin's voice was firm. "This zoo isn't set up to care for a growing grizzly. Most of the bears we have are adults who can't take care of themselves in the wild for one reason or another. Gus is a strong, healthy cub, and he'll be better off growing up in the forest." Justin leaned back on his chair and locked his hands around his neck. "We just can't feed him all the proper things he needs to stay in good shape."

"But—" Jessica began again. She had never felt so empty inside. "Justin, Gus needs me."

"Jessica." Justin looked her straight in the eyes. "You have done wonderful things for Gus, and you can be very proud of your work with him."

"But that's not what I mean," Jessica argued, trying to meet his gaze. "First he loses his mom, and then he loses me? I mean, that's totally unfair, you know it is!"

Justin put up his hand. "Gus doesn't have kids' emotions, Jessica. He might love you, but that isn't the same thing as a little kid loving its mother." He sighed. "And besides, you won't be able to put in these kind of hours forever. School will start, you'll have other things to do—"

"I'll quit them," Jessica promised. Suddenly none of her other activities seemed very important. "I'll be here every single day this summer, all day long, and when school starts, I'll be here by five minutes after three no matter what, I promise!"

Justin gave her a weary smile. "I wasn't finished. Gus is already growing. He's going to double his weight very soon, and then he'll double it again, and again, and again." He leaned forward earnestly. "When he's as big as a small car, you won't want to cuddle him any more."

"I *will* want to," Jessica protested, running her fingers through Gus's fur.

"I hear you. But the bottom line," Justin went on, "is that Gus can't be here forever. The wildlife department is responsible for him, and if he's healthy—which he is—he's got to go back to the wild. His visit was only temporary."

Temporary. A little switch clicked in Jessica's mind. She could almost hear Justin talking yesterday. "Blah blah blah blah temporary."

Jessica burst into tears. The bundle in her lap stirred.

"Jessica, I know you're upset." Justin leaned forward. "But Gus has to go home on Saturday. Tell you what. You can stay here as long as you like tonight, and as long as you like tomorrow, so you can say a proper good-bye."

Jessica cried harder. Gus growled and jerked to his feet. Pressing his cheek against hers, he began to moan, too.

Justin looked embarrassed. "I'll be back in a little while," he said gently, leaving the office.

Jessica sobbed into Gus's fur, and he whimpered. "I know. It's not fair, is it?" she asked him through her tears. "Nobody gets it. How do they expect me to just give you up?"

The party should be a blast, Bruce thought, putting out extra water for some of the larger birds. It was late Thursday afternoon, almost time for the interns' pizza party. "At least it better be, to make hanging out with you guys worth it," he told the birds.

"Eeep, eeep, eeep!" Drumstick, growing larger and less fluffy every day, hopped along adoringly behind him.

"Oh, you get out of here," Bruce commanded. He sloshed some of the water from his bucket onto the baby chick.

"Eeep!" Drumstick protested. But she didn't go away.

Bruce looked anxiously up to the top of the aviary where the predators sat. A monster of an eagle was hovering just above a craggy branch. Its beak looked at least three feet long, and sharp as a nail. A few hawks and buzzards flew lazily around the cage. All of them seemed to be staring directly at him.

He winced.

Eagles have awesome eyesight, he reminded himself. He wondered if they could see right into his heart and know how scared he was.

Something tugged at his coveralls. Bruce looked down to see Drumstick pulling at a loose thread. "Cut it out," he said impatiently, grabbing the little bird and tossing her across the aviary. "Eeep!" she cried when she landed.

Bruce glanced up again.

The predators above him were staring even more intently than before.

"I'm Elizabeth Wakefield, and they've just let me out of the monkey house."

Elizabeth nervously clutched the podium as laughter floated up from the audience. She was the final intern to deliver her speech at the preparty assembly that evening. She checked her notes and continued. "I've been working at the zoo for my internship, and I've noticed a lot of similarities between the monkeys and some of the kids in this school."

"Hey!" Bruce called out from the front row, setting his elbows heavily on both chair armrests.

"For instance, I've learned that monkeys are show-offs," Elizabeth went on with a pointed glance at Bruce.

"Chee, chee, chee!"

Someone can imitate a monkey pretty well, Elizabeth thought with surprise. *That sounded almost like—*

Elizabeth went pale.

There, at the back of the auditorium, she could see a very familiar little gray face.

"Spanky!" she shouted, dropping her notes and dashing down the aisle after him.

All at once the auditorium was in an uproar. "It's a monkey!" Brian Boyd shouted, wriggling out of his seat.

"Help!" Ellen Riteman screamed and jumped up onto her chair.

Jerry McAllister darted into the aisle toward Spanky, slipped, and fell headlong to the floor. "Grab him!" he shouted.

"I'm trying!" Elizabeth called back. She headed for the doorway, trying to cut Spanky off before he could make an escape. "Somebody shut the door!"

At the very back of the auditorium, Mandy Miller tugged the handle of the huge metal door. "It's stuck!" she shouted.

"Try again!" Elizabeth yelled back. Out of the corner of her eye, she could see kids jumping all over the place. Jerry was back on his feet again. This time he was approaching Spanky from behind. "Get him!" Elizabeth yelled.

Bruce vaulted over a row of seats and headed up the aisle behind Elizabeth. "You hit him low, I'll hit him high!" he called to Jerry. But at the last moment, Spanky darted to the left, and Jerry and Bruce grabbed only each other.

"Quiet!" Mr. Seigel, the science teacher, yelled at the top of his lungs.

"Chee, chee!" Spanky clambered up a wall and jumped confidently to a light fixture. Then he dropped onto the back of Ellen Riteman's neck.

"Aaaaah!" Ellen screamed.

With a whisk of his tail, Spanky darted to the ground and started dashing crazily beneath seats.

"Aaaaah!" Ellen screamed even louder. Lashing her arms to the left and right, she socked Jerry squarely in the nose. He fell crashing to the floor, howling with pain.

"Put your feet down, everyone!" Donald Zwerdling commanded from the stage. "If he comes near—"

"If he comes near, we'll bag that sucker!" Brian cried.

"Don't hurt him!" Elizabeth insisted, worried at the thought of Spanky underneath all those feet. "He's—"

"Chee, chee, chee!" Spanky called insistently. Elizabeth blinked. Somehow he'd gotten through ten rows of chairs—and now he was heading for the door!

"Mandy!" she shouted frantically.

"I still can't close the door!" Mandy yelled back. She was on her hands and knees, jiggling the lock.

"Aaaaah!" Ellen screamed.

"Owwww!" Jerry moaned.

Spanky scampered toward the door and swung himself up over a row of tables. "Grab him!" Elizabeth cried desperately. In the corridor she saw a man walking quickly toward the auditorium. "Sir!" she called, her voice frantic.

The man walked through the open door. He paused and blinked, and Elizabeth saw in a flash that he was delivering the pizzas for the party. "Is this where—"

At that moment, Spanky dived off the table and

was on top of him. The deliveryman's eyes widened with terror. "Get him off me!" he cried, dropping several boxes of pizza as he flattened himself against the wall.

"Chee, chee, chee!" Spanky cried. Before anyone could make a move, he had grabbed a box of pizza and was out the door.

Jessica tossed and turned that night for what seemed like hours. She'd been with Gus till eight-thirty, when the night keepers had finally made her leave, and had missed the interns' assembly and pizza party.

At last Jessica dropped off into a fitful sleep. Her dreams were full of bears—big bears and little bears, brown bears and black bears. Justin's car flashed into her dreams, too, with its bear bumper stickers: Take A Bear To Lunch, I'm A Party Bear, and Bear Crossing, which showed bear cubs wearing backpacks, like little kids going to school.

At three o'clock in the morning, Jessica woke up suddenly. The images from her dreams were still dancing in her head.

Backpacks. Bears. "That's it!" she said aloud, her voice echoing in the dark room.

Sixteen

"You're here awfully early this morning, Jessica." Justin watched her from the door to Gus's cage.

It was Friday morning, and Jessica had awakened extra early today. "Mmmm," she said noncommittally, rolling the tennis ball to Gus. Her heart was beating furiously.

"I know you're upset about yesterday," Justin continued gently. "I hope you're feeling better today?"

"Mmmm," Jessica said again. She watched as Gus batted the ball back to her with his paw.

"I hope that means yes." Justin wiped his forehead. "Um—you've really been a great intern, Jessica, and I'm sorry to see your time with us come to an end."

"Yeah, well," Jessica responded. Not daring to look at Justin, she picked up the ball again and swatted it back to Gus.

Justin turned to leave. "This your backpack here,

Jessica?" Jessica looked up and swallowed hard, trying not to show any signs of nervousness. "That? Oh. That's my brother's," she said with a careless wave of her hand toward Steven's humongous camping backpack that she had sort of borrowed that morning.

Justin grinned. "It's a nice one. And, by the way, you're welcome to come with me tomorrow while I take Gus back to—you know where. I'd clear it with your parents. We'll leave at nine o'clock. Interested?"

Jessica looked up at Justin. There was the ghost of a smile on her face. "Thanks, Justin," she said slowly, "but I don't think so."

She gave Gus an extra-large hug.

Because if my plan works, Gus won't be going any-where!

Three o'clock. Bruce heaved a huge sigh of relief. "I'm out of here!" he shouted, pushing Drumstick away. The little bird landed with an injured squawk.

Bruce snickered. His internship was over. Whistling happily to himself, he saluted the predators up at the top of the aviary. "Bruce 1, Raptors 0!" he shouted, shaking his fist at them.

Bruce ducked out of the aviary and went to the locker room to change. He unzipped his coveralls and yanked them off for the last time. It actually hadn't been that bad, he told himself as he reached into the locker. "Patman takes on birds and sur-vives!" he said, pretending to announce it into a microphone. "Film at eleven." A feeling of satisfaction spread through his body.

As he started pulling on his blue jeans, he heard a distinct noise from the aviary. "Eeep, eeep, eeep!"

Bruce rolled his eyes. Drumstick again. "Aw, shut up already!" he groaned.

"Eeep, eeep!"

With one leg in his jeans, Bruce held still for a moment and frowned. That cry hadn't sounded quite right somehow. It was louder than usual, and it seemed to be coming from up high. *Oh well. Who cares.* He reached out his leg—

"Eeep, eeep, eeeeeeeep!"

Startled, Bruce let his jeans fall to the floor. He walked to the screened window and squinted to see out. *It's not like I care,* he told himself. *I just want to know what's going on, that's all.*

His gaze traveled over to the aviary. His head bent backward—farther, farther—to look up to the very top of a pole. Bruce's jaw dropped. Drumstick was sitting on a wooden beam attached to the pole. "How did you get up there?" he demanded, staring in surprise at the little bird.

She's gotta be a hundred feet in the air!

"Eeep!" Drumstick complained.

Bruce leaned forward for a better look. His stomach knotted.

Circling only a few feet above Drumstick were some of the largest raptors in the entire world.

"Drumstick!" At top speed, Bruce dashed out of the locker room. "Drumstick!" He looked frantically around for Melissa, for Pam Moreland, for anyone who could help. "Help!"

There was no answer. Drumstick only clucked louder.

"Drumstick!" Bruce shielded his eyes against the afternoon sun. "Come down right now!"

The predators tightened their circle around Drumstick. Biting his lip, Bruce saw that one bird was almost directly above the chick's fuzzy little head.

"Well, I'm going now." Justin walked over to where Jessica was playing with Gus.

"OK," Jessica said. She bounced Gus in her lap. "Bye."

"Hope to see you again real soon," Justin said. "And if you change your mind about tomorrow?" Pretending to talk into a phone, he made dialing motions with his finger.

Jessica nodded.

"Good luck," Justin said. "And I *am* sorry."

Jessica waited until his footsteps were gone. In the distance she almost thought she could hear Justin's Jeep starting up. Her eyes sparkled.

It was time to put her plan into action.

I guess I don't really have a choice, Bruce thought miserably. He willed his knees to stop knocking. Reaching out, he steadied himself against the pole.

Well, he thought, licking his lips, *here goes nothing!*

Slowly he began to climb.

* * *

"Shh," Jessica warned Gus as she pushed him gently into Steven's huge backpack. She was awfully glad she'd taught Gus to play hide-and-seek. "You're hiding," she informed him. "So don't make a sound, OK?"

Gus growled agreeably.

Jessica buckled the backpack shut, hoping Gus would soon go to sleep in the darkness. Then she hoisted the pack to her back, wincing a little at the weight. Then Jessica locked the cage behind her and headed for the exit.

Stupid bird, Bruce thought as he shinnied his way up the pole. How could Drumstick be so dense, getting into a position like this? Especially when no one else was around. Especially where there weren't any ladders.

But he couldn't let Drumstick be eaten.

Could he?

Bruce paused for breath and looked down. He'd come a long way. He glanced up and set his jaw. There was a long way to go.

A sudden motion distracted him. Startled, he saw a humongous vulture swooping right down toward Drumstick!

"Go away!" Bruce shouted at the top of his lungs. Digging his knees into the pole, he shook both fists menacingly at the vulture. "Go home! Shoo!"

The vulture pulled out of its dive and resumed circling. *Phew*, Bruce thought, wiping sweat from his brow. But he didn't know how much longer he could keep the birds away. The sky was thick with predators.

Bruce grimaced and climbed higher.

Almost out of here, Jessica told herself. A few feet ahead of her was the gate to the zoo—and just beyond that the brick wall she'd leaned against when she'd first found out she'd be working with the bears. It seemed like years ago.

"Jessica!"

Startled, Jessica whirled around. Mrs. Tomlinson, the head zookeeper, was standing in front of the door to her office. "Leaving so soon?" Mrs. Tomlinson called out, a friendly smile on her face.

"Um—yeah," Jessica stammered, her heart racing. She could feel Gus shifting his weight inside the backpack. "I had a fun time, though."

"Thanks for all your help with Gus," Mrs. Tomlinson said.

Jessica gulped and tried to grin. "Um—no problem."

"I must admit, I had my doubts about you on the first day," Mrs. Tomlinson went on. "But Justin tells me you've been terrific."

"Yeah, well, it was fun," Jessica said hastily. "And don't worry about Gus. He's all curled up now—nice and cozy. Bye!" Walking as fast as she dared, she headed through the gates of the zoo.

Just a few more feet to go, Bruce told himself firmly. His head swam as he glanced down. The ground seemed miles away, and his muscles were straining with the effort of the climb.

Bruce looked once more toward the top of the pole—and saw three birds diving down, down, down toward Drumstick, their wings outspread, their claws sharp and gleaming in the brilliant sunshine.

Bruce's chest tightened. Summoning all his courage, he thwacked his fist against the metal. "Stop!" he shouted, using every ounce of lung power. "Stop it! Leave her alone!"

Slowly, reluctantly, the three birds swooped off in the other direction.

Bruce's mouth felt completely dry. He didn't dare look down, and he didn't dare look up. Instead, he gazed at the frightened chick now almost near enough to touch.

"Eeep!" Drumstick saw him. She began to toddle happily along the narrow plank.

"Oh, no you don't! Stay right where you are! That's a hundred-foot drop-off we're talking about here." Bruce wasn't about to let Drumstick walk any farther on those unsteady legs. He dragged his bare chest across the top of the pole. Its jagged edge scratched him badly, but he held on.

Balancing with one arm and one leg, he stretched as far toward Drumstick as he could. His fingers reached—groped—and finally grabbed. His heart hammering, Bruce pulled the little chick safely against his chest.

"Got you!" he whispered, feeling faint. "You're safe with me!"

And two feet overhead, the raptors dropped back onto their perches.

Seventeen

"You total idiot," Bruce whispered, holding Drumstick against his chest as he started the long climb down. "Do you know just how idiotic you are?"

"Eeep," Drumstick said mournfully, trying to burrow into Bruce's armpit.

Bruce took a deep breath. *I can't believe I risked my stupid life for this dumb bird,* he thought, looking up to see how far down he'd come. Up above, the raptors were sitting motionless on their perches. "I could have fallen," he muttered to the little chick, grasping her a little more tightly just in case she decided to try to jump. "I could have bashed my brains out. I could have been killed!"

"Eeep," Drumstick agreed.

Bruce sighed loudly. "You'd just better appreciate it."

Drumstick wiggled her wings. Her downy fluff

tickled Bruce's chest. He sighed. "I mean, not that I would have wanted—" He bit his lip as an image rose in his mind: the vulture, its sharp claws glistening against the blue sky, scudding down and tearing Drumstick into bloody pieces. He shook his head, then cleared his throat. "Well, you know."

"Who knows what?" a voice behind him asked.

Startled, Bruce lost his balance. Half jumping, half falling the last couple of feet, he stumbled heavily against a wooden shed, keeping Drumstick wrapped protectively in the crook of his arm. To his amazement, Melissa stood in front of him.

"Oh—nothing," he said with as much dignity as he could muster. "I was just—you know—doing some stuff."

"In your underpants?" Melissa stared curiously into Bruce's face.

In my under—oh, good grief. Bruce's mouth hung open. He had completely forgotten that he'd never finished changing into his clothes. He looked around frantically for something to hide behind. "Oh, well, you know." He slouched against the wall of the shed and forced a laugh. "When you gotta do something, you gotta—um—you gotta do it."

A smile played at the corners of Melissa's mouth.

Bruce felt himself turn red. *She's laughing at me,* he thought. All at once, he realized how completely embarrassing this whole thing was. Here he was, practically naked and scratched up and clutching a stupid little bird in front of the girl he'd been wanting to impress for weeks. *I look a total and complete—*

"Bruce, you're a hero." Melissa was beaming now.

Bruce blinked. "A what? I am?"

Melissa took a step closer. "I saw the whole thing. You rescued Drumstick."

Bruce's mind reeled. "I—you—?"

"For a person who's scared to death of birds, you sure were brave," Melissa added.

Bruce stared. If he hadn't known better, he would have sworn that Melissa was giving him a warm smile. "Did you say—brave?" he asked weakly.

Melissa nodded. "And you're also wonderful." Taking another step, she leaned forward and kissed Bruce on the cheek.

"What's that noise?" Elizabeth asked that night at dinner, putting her fork down.

Jessica's heart skipped a beat. She'd managed to get Gus home without too many weird looks from strangers. She'd managed to teach him not to bounce on her bed. But now there was no mistaking the low moaning coming from her bedroom. "Noise?" she said as calmly as she could, looking around. "What noise? I don't hear a thing."

"Then you must be going deaf," Steven remarked.

Jessica cringed as the moaning grew louder.

Mrs. Wakefield frowned. "I think it's coming from your room, Jessica."

"Sounds like a wild animal." Steven narrowed his eyes and stared hard at his sister.

Jessica gulped. There seemed to be no way around it. "Oh, *that* noise!" she said as brightly as she could. "I left my radio on, that's all. It's a new pop group."

"Pop group?" Mr. Wakefield raised his eyebrows. "Pop music has sure gone downhill since we were kids, don't you think, Alice?" he asked his wife.

"It's an alternative-fusion–world beat kind of thing," Jessica added carelessly. She shot her brother a look. "You wouldn't have heard of them, Steven."

Steven's eyes flashed. "Oh, yeah? For your information, they sound a lot like—um—Four Howling Dogs." He smiled triumphantly.

Jessica shook her head as Gus's moaning grew louder and decidedly less musical. "For *your* information, they're called the, um, the Bear Necessities." She folded her arms with satisfaction. "But I wouldn't expect you to have heard of *them.*"

Steven snorted. "The Bare Necessities, huh? Of *course* I've heard of them!"

"OK, Gus," Jessica murmured at nine o'clock that night. She changed into her nightgown while Gus lay sleepily against the pillow. "Almost bedtime, all right?"

Gus yawned. Jessica wondered if bears slept through the night at whatever age Gus was. She hoped so. "You'll be sleeping under the desk," she told him softly, laying out a few old doll blankets for him on the floor. It was the only place that wasn't a total mess.

Gus grunted. Drowsily he reached out and gave Jessica a lick on her face.

So far, so good, Jessica thought. No one had noticed that Gus was around. She'd smuggled four peanut butter sandwiches up to him after dinner, and he'd eaten them all. Everything was—

There was a knock on the door.

"Who is it?" Jessica swung around to the door, all her senses on guard. There wasn't time to dump Gus in the closet, so she quickly covered him with her bedspread and hoped he wouldn't move. "Who's there?"

"It's me." Mrs. Wakefield's voice carried through the door. "May I come in?"

"Um—yeah." Jessica swallowed hard. She plastered a smile across her face and opened the door. "What's up, Mom? I was just about to go to bed."

Mrs. Wakefield smiled back. "I just wanted to tell you that my clients, the Tweeds, are coming over tomorrow—so please be on your best behavior."

"Sure, Mom." *And for that you almost gave me a heart attack?* Jessica thought, shaking her head. She pretended to yawn. "So I'll see you in the morning, OK?"

"Of course." Mrs. Wakefield leaned forward and gave Jessica a kiss. Her eyes traveled to the lump in the bed. "What's in there?"

Jessica gulped. "Um, my teddy bear, Gus."

Mrs. Wakefield looked faintly surprised. "I thought you said you were too old for teddy bears."

"Me?" Jessica hoped she looked bewildered. "Oh, no, I'm not too old at all."

Eighteen

◇

Jessica opened one eye on Saturday morning and peeked at the clock. The first digit, glowing red, was a 9. *Yes!* She lifted her head a little bit farther to see the rest of the numbers. "9:43," she murmured aloud. "All right!"

Gus had officially missed his ride.

"You hear that, Gus?" she called softly. "You don't have to go back to that dumb old forest. You can stay right here!"

She listened, but Gus didn't respond. Squinting to get the cobwebs out of her eyes, Jessica peered toward Gus's bed beneath the desk. The blankets had clearly been slept in, but there was no bear anywhere in sight.

Jessica quickly glanced around her room—and caught her breath.

The door to her bedroom was open.

Don't panic, Jessica told herself. *He's probably just*

outside the door. She tossed off her covers, but before she even stepped out of bed, she heard strange noises coming from downstairs. Some chattering. A scream. And—a growl.

A very familiar growl.

Her heart thundering, Jessica jumped out of bed and barreled out the bedroom door.

Jessica dashed into the kitchen at top speed. Coming to an abrupt halt, she stared—and stared—and stared.

There, in the center of the room, was Gus, looking toward the garbage can with a hungry expression on his face. Curled behind the garbage can was a very thin man. "Get him away from me!" he was shouting, his hands flailing in Gus's general direction.

Jessica was about to step forward when she heard an ear-piercing wail behind her.

"Help! Oh, help!" Jessica turned to see a woman clutching the kitchen counter. Above her a monkey swung down from the light fixture and dropped a grape into the woman's huge hair.

"Spanky!" Elizabeth, fully dressed, was standing on the kitchen table. "You stop that!"

"He's going to bite my head off!" the very thin man shouted, a note of panic in his voice.

"Mr. Tweed, please!" Mrs. Wakefield begged. She got between the man and the bear cub. "He won't bite," she assured him. She drew in her breath as Gus yawned mightily. "I think," she added quickly.

"Chee, chee," Spanky chattered from the top of the refrigerator.

"Spanky!" Elizabeth exclaimed desperately.

"Come down right now!" Mr. Wakefield ordered, swatting the monkey with a broom.

I'm dreaming, Jessica told herself. *I have to be dreaming.* "Take that!" Mr. Tweed shouted, pushing the garbage can over. It fell with a crash at Gus's feet.

Jessica felt her body stiffen with anger. No doubt about it—she was awake, and she was watching real life. "Gus!" she shouted frantically.

"Jessica!" Mr. Wakefield sounded furious. "What is the meaning of this?"

Jessica knew she ought to grab Gus, but she couldn't seem to make her feet move forward. Gus growled happily and began to nose through the garbage in search of good leftovers.

"Chee, chee, chee!" Spanky danced around just out of Elizabeth's reach.

"A zoo, a zoo," Mrs. Tweed moaned. "My interior decorator keeps a zoo!" She tugged at her dress, which had somehow gotten caught in a drawer. There was a tearing sound.

"Mrs. Wakefield!" Mr. Tweed's face looked bright red. "You'll be hearing from our lawyer!" He kicked viciously at the garbage can and missed. Jessica watched, astonished, as his legs slipped out from under him and he fell with a crash to the kitchen floor. "Help!" he shouted as Gus lumbered over and began sniffing him. "He'll eat me alive!"

"Chee, chee, chee!" In an instant Spanky opened the refrigerator, grabbed an egg, and threw it at Mr. Tweed. It broke, and yolk spattered all over the thin man's fancy suit.

"Kill him!" Mr. Tweed screamed, shielding his head with his arm.

"Don't you dare!" Jessica's feet were finally in motion. She strode forward and seized Gus. "Don't you know anything?" she demanded, staring down at the cowering Mr. Tweed. "Baby bears won't hurt you! All he wants is a little love!"

Mr. Tweed blinked at her icily.

Jessica could feel Gus's tiny heart racing. "You ought to be ashamed of yourself!" she told Mr. Tweed angrily. "Now you've scared him, and he only wanted to be friends!"

Jessica turned at the sound of some shuffling behind her. With a heave, her father was bringing a heavy wooden crate down over Spanky's head. But at the last moment, the little monkey wiggled away and darted for the screen door. Whooping with joy, he disappeared into the morning sunshine.

"Not again!" Elizabeth whimpered, sinking against the kitchen counter and covering her face.

"I give up."

Elizabeth choked down a tear. She was sitting in Madeleine's office at the zoo a little later that morning. "I've been chasing Spanky for days now," she went on, blowing her nose, "and I keep seeing him, and no matter what, I can't seem to catch him."

"You can't blame yourself for not catching him," Madeleine said consolingly. "Monkeys are—"

"—very intelligent," Elizabeth finished for her. "I know that now. I didn't believe you at first, but now I know the truth." She thought back to that horrible scene earlier that morning. "I mean, I can't figure out how he even got into my house."

Madeleine smiled. "Through an open window, maybe. Or possibly some other way. It wouldn't be too hard for a clever monkey like Spanky."

Elizabeth took a deep breath and tried to smile. "Whatever. I guess monkeys are about the most intelligent animals in the whole world."

Madeleine was about to say something when there was a sudden knock on the window. Turning to see, Elizabeth caught sight of a small gray figure hovering on the outside of the windowsill.

Elizabeth could only stare as Spanky waved to her. His red lips parted in a wide grin.

Elizabeth burst into fresh tears. "You win," she told him. She wasn't even going to try to catch him this time. Instead, she walked out of the office and headed for her bike.

"Is that you, Elizabeth?" Mr. Wakefield asked gruffly when Elizabeth arrived back home.

"Uh-huh," Elizabeth answered morosely. She knew it wasn't her fault that she couldn't catch Spanky, but she kept blaming herself anyway.

"You're supposed to call Madeleine at the zoo," her father told her. "She says it's important."

Elizabeth frowned. "But I was just—" she began, when suddenly the phone rang. Curious, Elizabeth picked up the receiver. "Hello?" she said.

"Elizabeth!" Madeleine sounded breathless. "I wondered if maybe you didn't get my message."

Elizabeth sighed. "Yeah, I—"

"The most amazing thing happened just after you left," Madeleine broke in. "Spanky's back!"

Elizabeth felt her shoulders sag. "I know, Madeleine. He was outside the window. I saw him."

"No, I mean *back* back," Madeleine went on. "In the monkey house back. He turned himself in!"

Elizabeth's eyes lit up. "He *what?*"

"He came to the door of the monkey cage and begged to be let back in," Madeleine explained excitedly. "And the other monkeys were so glad to see him, too. They've been giving each other high fives ever since, if you can believe it."

Elizabeth let out all her breath. "You know what, Madeleine?" she asked. "After chasing Spanky for a week, I believe it!"

"You don't really expect us to believe that Spanky did the whole thing just to teach you a lesson, do you?" Amy asked, taking a long sip of her milk shake.

"But he *did*," Elizabeth insisted. "He ran away to show me how smart monkeys were. When I finally admitted it he gave up." She took a bite of her ice cream. "Monkeys are incredibly smart, you know."

Maria patted Elizabeth's shoulder. "Don't forget, monkeys aren't human. They're just animals."

Elizabeth started to speak. Then she stopped and smiled. *I guess I had to see it for myself,* she thought. *Maybe they do too.*

"Speaking of animals," Mr. Casey said from

behind the counter, "do you think I can get those two lovebirds out of that corner booth before dinnertime? They've been there all afternoon!"

Elizabeth spun around on her stool to look. *Well, what do you know!* she thought, giving a low whistle. There were Melissa and Bruce, gazing dreamily at each other's faces.

"I don't know if you'll get them out of here, Mr. Casey," she told him with a grin. "But when you call them love*birds*—I think you're exactly right!"

"Oh, Bruce," Melissa sighed, staring deep into his eyes.

"Oh, Melissa," Bruce sighed back, hardly daring to believe his incredibly good luck.

"I always thought you were kind of cute," Melissa went on, "but after you saved Drumstick, I found out you were brave and strong and caring, too."

"Yeah, well," Bruce said modestly. He let go of her hand long enough to push his empty ice cream soda glass away. "After the first week at the zoo, I didn't think you'd ever go for me," he admitted, reaching for her hand again. It felt nice and warm.

"Well, after you saved Drumstick, how could I have any doubts?" Melissa murmured.

Bruce thought back to yesterday afternoon. He could see himself at the bottom of the pole, scratched and in his underwear, clutching that little chick. Not exactly a walking advertisement for a macho guy, but somehow—

"Oh, Bruce," Melissa whispered again, clutching his hand even tighter.

Well, Bruce told himself as he looked deeply into her eyes, *it just goes to show you.*

You never can tell what a woman will like!

Nineteen

On Sunday morning, Jessica woke up early, put on her zoo uniform, and shuffled down to the kitchen. *My last day with Gus*, she thought sadly. *My very last day.*

She made herself a frozen waffle and thought about everything that had happened yesterday morning. Incredibly, the Tweeds hadn't fired Mrs. Wakefield—or sued her, either. Instead, they'd settled for an apology and some new clothes. "My, oh my!" Mrs. Tweed had said heartily after it was all over. "Why, we hadn't had such a time since our little Felicia's eighth birthday party!"

As she poured syrup on her waffle, Jessica's mind flashed back to the serious talk she'd had with her parents yesterday morning. To the horrible phone call she'd had to make to Justin. How Justin had arrived, stern and angry, to pick up Gus. And how, finally, Justin and her parents had begun to understand why she'd done what she'd done. In the end, they told her she could go with Justin today to find the best place for Gus to live.

And as much as Jessica hated to admit it, Justin's arguments were actually making a little bit of sense now. It was hard work keeping a growing bear in your room. She ticked reasons off on her fingers. *He is kind of big—and he really did scare the Tweeds out of their wits—and he ate way more food than I could possibly afford on my allowance—*

She stopped and shook her head. *But on the other hand, he's* Gus, she thought. Her heart ached already.

There was a sharp honk from a Jeep outside.

"Coming!" Jessica put her plate in the sink and dashed out the door to meet Justin and Gus.

"I know how much you love him," Justin said a few hours later.

The Jeep was chugging up a steep mountain road, but Jessica barely saw the scenery. Her eyes filled with tears as she gently rocked a sleepy Gus in her arms. "I—I just hate to give him up," she said softly, careful not to awaken him.

"Maybe he'll spend more time with us again, later on in his life," Justin continued, "but now he's best off in the wild."

"I—" Jessica swallowed. "I know." And she really did know. She stared intently at the gentle rise and fall of Gus's chest, trying to commit his every movement to memory.

Justin rounded a curve and threw the car into a

lower gear. "This is where he ought to be. Just look at this landscape!"

Jessica dried her eyes against Gus's fur and looked out the window. Beautiful green hills rolled out to meet the sky, and the air smelled clean and fresh. In the distance a lone hawk circled a grove of tall pine trees. Jessica took a deep breath. "I guess it's better than a cramped old cage," she admitted.

Justin grinned and steered the Jeep onto a narrow dirt road. "There's a pretty little stream back here," he said. "He'd like that, don't you think?"

Jessica blinked back tears. Suddenly she could see Gus in her mind's eye, an all–grown-up Gus, lumbering out into the rushing water and catching a salmon or two in a thick paw. "Yes," she said, swallowing hard. "He'll like that."

She stroked Gus's fur and waited.

"Here we are." Justin pulled the key out of the ignition and gestured to the scenery in front of him. "What do you think?"

They were at the very end of the little road. "It's—beautiful," Jessica admitted, staring out at the wilderness that seemed to go on forever. In the distance she could hear the roar of a creek running down the hillside.

Justin opened the door. "Let's go."

"Wait." In Jessica's arms, Gus was stretching. He was waking up. Jessica watched him yawn and slowly open his mouth. A change seemed to come over him as he sniffed the pure mountain air.

Grunting, he raised his nose and took a deep, deep breath.

Jessica sat absolutely motionless.

Lumbering onto his back legs, Gus propped his front paws against the open window and looked out across the hills. Then he hopped out the window and sat in the cool grass, turning around impatiently as though waiting for Jessica to follow.

Jessica grinned. She opened the door of the Jeep and walked out onto the grass.

Justin nodded to her. "Let's walk down the path a little ways," he suggested.

"OK." Jessica was glad for the chance to spend just a little more time with Gus. She bent down and pointed toward the trail, feeling Gus's soft warm body against hers. "How about it, boy?"

Gus didn't need to be asked twice. Wriggling to his feet, he bounded on ahead.

Jessica looked at the beautiful wilderness all around her. The clear, cool water of the stream cascaded down among the shiny rocks. Gold and purple wildflowers dotted the meadow, and Jessica could see trees for shade and shelter at the edge of the grass.

"Look." Justin breathed deeply. "The perfect spot for a growing bear."

Jessica nodded, feeling the tears about to come.

Gus grunted happily and waddled off to explore the stream. Jessica bit her lip as she watched him go. "Can we stay here for a while?" she asked hopefully.

Justin shook his head. "We aren't doing him any favors by hanging around."

"Oh." Jessica swallowed hard. "Then—can I—you know—say good-bye?" she asked in a very small voice.

"Of course." Justin patted Jessica on the shoulder. "Just make it quick, OK?"

Jessica nodded. Taking a few steps forward, she watched Gus balancing carefully on the rocks. His sleek fur coat already looked sleeker than it had yesterday, she thought, and he seemed less like a teddy bear and more like a real bear all the time. "Gus?" she asked hesitantly.

Gus turned. Lumbering off the rocks, he scampered to her side and looked up at her with his watery brown eyes.

Jessica reached down and gave him a huge hug. Gus nuzzled in as usual. *For the last time*, Jessica thought, no longer able to hold back her tears.

Gus licked her face with his sandpapery tongue.

"I'll always remember you, Gus," Jessica said. Her heart felt as if it were breaking. She buried her face deep inside his fur.

"Jessica." Justin's voice was gentle but firm.

"I know." Reluctantly, Jessica pulled her face away from the bear cub. "Run and play, Gus," she whispered. "Just remember I'll always love you." Letting go at last, she set Gus down and watched as he scampered over to the edge of the woods.

"Good-bye, Gus," she said, her lip trembling.

Gus sat down and grunted at her questioningly.

"He wants me to come, too," Jessica whispered

to Justin, almost hoping that he would tell her to go off into the forest with the little bear.

"I know." Justin smiled and patted Jessica's back. "But it's time to go."

Jessica nodded, and as if in a dream, she followed Justin slowly down the path. "Will he remember me?" she asked as they headed around the hillside.

"Forever," Justin assured her.

Jessica managed a weak smile. "Can I come to visit?" she asked, afraid that she already knew the answer.

"No." Justin shook his head. "Bears and people just don't mix. Lots of people hate and fear bears, you know."

"Hate a bear?" Jessica stared uncomprehendingly at Justin. "Who in the world would hate a bear?"

Justin's eyes twinkled. "I can't imagine."

They rounded a bend on the trail. Jessica looked behind her for a last glimpse of Gus. He was sitting straight up on his back legs, nose in the air, breathing deeply the cool, sweet mountain air. As Jessica watched, he reached up and pulled a berry off a nearby bush.

He's come home, Jessica thought, happy and miserable at the same time. *He's home.*

And then the tears began again.

"So here we are, back where it all began," Justin said awkwardly a few hours later. They were back at the zoo once more. He turned off the engine and faced Jessica. "Um—thanks for everything."

"Thank *you*," Jessica said. And she meant it. "Without you, I wouldn't have gotten to—" She paused. "Well—you know."

"Forget it." Justin looked embarrassed. He jerked his thumb toward the locker rooms. "Just go get changed and get out of here," he added with a wry smile.

"Actually—" Jessica hesitated. Sniffing her overalls, she found that they smelled strongly of her favorite scent in the world—Gus. She breathed in deeply. "I had a question."

Justin looked at her curiously. "What is it?"

"Um—" Jessica flashed him a shy smile. "Would it be OK if I kept my uniform?"

Bantam Books in the SWEET VALLEY TWINS series.
Ask your bookseller for the books you have missed.

Sweet Valley Twins Super Editions

Sweet Valley Twins Super Chiller Editions

Sweet Valley Twins Magna Editions

SIGN UP FOR THE SWEET VALLEY HIGH® FAN CLUB!

Hey, girls! Get all the gossip on Sweet Valley High's® most popular teenagers when you join our fantastic Fan Club! As a member, you'll get all of this really cool stuff:

- Membership Card with your own personal Fan Club ID number
- A Sweet Valley High® Secret Treasure Box
- Sweet Valley High® Stationery
- Official Fan Club Pencil (for secret note writing!)
- Three Bookmarks
- A "Members Only" Door Hanger
- Two Skeins of J. & P. Coats® Embroidery Floss with flower barrette instruction leaflet
- Two editions of *The Oracle* newsletter
- Plus exclusive Sweet Valley High® product offers, special savings, contests, and much more!

- -

Be the first to find out what Jessica & Elizabeth Wakefield are up to by joining the Sweet Valley High® Fan Club for the one-year membership fee of only $6.25 each for U.S. residents, $8.25 for Canadian residents (U.S. currency). Includes shipping & handling.

Send a check or money order (do not send cash) made payable to "Sweet Valley High® Fan Club" along with this form to:

SWEET VALLEY HIGH® FAN CLUB, BOX 3919-B, SCHAUMBURG, IL 60168-3919

NAME _____
(Please print clearly)

ADDRESS _____

CITY_____ STATE _____ ZIP_____
(Required)

AGE_____ BIRTHDAY_____ / _____ / _____